Eb

CW00384578

Cèdric Daurio

PROLOGUE

He finally left the baggage claim area of the Kennedy Airport of New York dragging his own suitcase and another with casual clothes that Fatima had asked him to bring, since she had taken with her only the African costumes tailored to the meetings that she was going to attend.

First he recognized in the huge hall was the impressive and unmistakable figure of Malik, the refugee from the Central African Republic who had already saved them from the intrigues of hostile actors in their previous stay in the city.

Cristian hugged him affectionately surprising the big man characterized by a more cautious attitude. To his embarrassment Malik took charge of the luggage without the slightest effort.

"The Princess will meet with you at the hotel" He said recalling to Cristian the rather royal treatment given to his wife. "Today she is having a meeting arranged at the last minute and could not come to the airport as she wanted to."

"The history of my life as a married man." Thought Cristian.

Already in the car asked Malik if he had any news about clashes between different African ethnic groups on their continent and if they had had repercussions among the expatriate groups in New York.

"In Africa, conflicts have moved to the Central African Republic, my country, and possibly in the near future will arrive in Nigeria. Here the situation is calmer that when you and the Princess were a couple of years ago but we cannot lower our guard."

These words reminded Cristian that one of Malik´s the functions was acting as a custodian of Fatima while she was in the city.

When the African parked his car in front of the hotel Cristian was surprised to see that it was the same in which Fatima and he had first met. A wave of memories invaded his mind and a knot formed in his throat but he refrained from making comments.

When they entered at the hotel Fatima had just arrived and they met in the lobby the woman threw herself in his arms in a completely unexpected attitude. Guests of the hotel looked askance at that woman richly dressed in her obvious ethnicity silk dress hugging a newcomer looking tired and dressing wrinkled clothes. Seeing the scene with the corner of his eye in a lobby mirror brought Christian even more emotions and they both whined for a second.

Malik cleared his throat to call them into reality and they separated with a certain embarrassment.

"It´s only a week since we last met." Cristian told his wife in a tone of false reproach.

"Why then you have red eyes?"

In fact what had worked in the encounter between the two was not the brief recent separation but all the vicissitudes that had occurred since they had left the hotel two years before with their joys and sufferings. No doubt this relatively brief period had transformed their lives in a deep and lasting way.

The woman had already obtained her key at the front desk and guided him towards her room.

"But... this is..." Sputtered Cristian.

"Yes, it is the same room that we were when we met. I spent several days in another but I ordered the Concierge to move me to it as soon as it was vacant.

The detail moved him again. He knew the value of symbols for his wife and her tenacity to achieve her purposes. Having obtained the same room spoke clearly of the importance Fatima granted the event when they had loved for the first time.

They entered the spacious room and the employee left the suitcases. She made him sit on the bed smiling and placed her arms around his neck.

"*Mon cher*, you don't know how long I have dreamed with this moment, to relive the most important stage of my life and to taste again its flavor.

CHAPTER 1

She had been contemplating him over breakfast in the spacious lounge on the ground floor of the hotel. She had seen him for the first time one week before, along with one of the older women whose sexual needs he was without a doubt satisfying. He didn't have the muscular and athletic appearance of other *gigolos* she had seen before but there was something in him that drew her mightily. Thin and very high, with an undisciplined but not very long blonde hair he had a somewhat fragile although manly appearance. His features were fine and correct and at the distance it seemed that his eyes were clear. He did not exceed much the twenty years.

The woman looked at him fixedly from her own table and finally managed that their eyes crossed. The young man realized that she was looking at him and he looked at her briefly but then surely by shyness he lowered his eyes.

"Insecure, odd trait in his profession." Thought Fatima. "I don´t think that it is by racial prejudice."

The woman had taken her decision and wouldn't reverse for a timid reaction of the young man. With natural elegance she rose from her table and turned resolutely to his. The eyes of the other guests, mostly men, stood in admiration of her magnificent silhouette causing the twitching in the ladies who accompanied them. Very tall and slender, with upright bust, narrow waist and prominent buttocks, her black skin shone with strange blue flashes. Her head and facial features were an excellent sample of typically African beauty in the fullness of life; her walk was feline and she seemed to slip into space with pure grace.

The young man noticed that the woman approached him and stirred simultaneously excited and restless in his chair. He was accustomed to more or less veiled female approaches but who was now approaching in no way resembled his usual clientele. He had already seen her at the hotel in previous days and her sight drew and disturbed him at the same time.

The woman stood in front of his table, and the man reacted by standing up and moving a chair so she could sit.

"Good manners, he is not from New York. I wonder where is he from." Wondered Fatima. After a few moments of shared silence they both began to speak in unison.

"We knew...?" He began saying.

"Why did you..." The lady temporarily interrupted her speech but finally imposed silence to the man, foretelling what their relations would be like from there on.

"Why did you turn your eyes away from me when we looked each other?" She asked

"I don't know, it was an instinctive reaction."

"Look at me now!"

Their eyes kept an intense look until each was dissolved on the other. The simple gesture of observing each other provided Fatima the information she needed. Without further preambles she told him.

"Follow me." Then she walked without looking back. The man with certain signs of embarrassment followed her in direction to the elevators. Several people made comments in a low voice and the concierge of the hotel discreetly grimaced to another guest.

They crossed the lobby and entered an elevator that was arrested. The lady pushed the 14th floor button.

The woman opened the door of the room 1421 and noting a hesitant attitude of the youngster took him by one arm and gently pulled him inside. Then she dragged him to the bed and then pushed forcing him to sit in it. In absolute silence she unbuttoned her dress revealing her magnificent black body. She wore long white stockings up to the thighs, a brief panty also white and a bra that barely contained her breasts. Without delay she placed her body close to him, then took his head and approached it with their hips, then broke the silence and ordered.

"Pull down my panties... with your teeth."

The man obediently took the edge of lace between his teeth and began the downward movement in the course of which his face slid over her black skin and soon contacted her short but not shaved pubic hair. Then he felt a sudden erection but continued with his task passing in front of her moist genitals. The movement went on until the brief garment was at the level of her thighs when he grabbed it in his hands and took it off her legs. Then he took the buttocks of the woman between his hands and got his face into her crotch. She set him aside with a sudden movement and pushed him placing him with his back on the bed, with his head hanging barely on the lateral edge of the mattress. Supporting one of her legs on the floor on one side of his head, and turning the other over the bed from the other side; she sat on his face putting in contact directly her sex with his lips.

Surprised but excited, the youngster began the task which was requested from him in such an obvious way. The woman pleased because her intentions had been well interpreted and accepted, began performing a soft rolling her hips while she aired unintelligible whispers.

The African began rocking more energetically and her groans almost inaudible at the beginning became louder and more frequent. After a few moments, however she found that in that position she could not reach the climax so repeatedly changed the relative position of her sex and his face. Finally, in the midst of an uncontrolled swing the woman had a deep and long orgasm.

Momentarily calmed her cravings she changed its stance kneeling on the pillows at the head of the bed with her hands resting on the wall and her legs bent at a right angle. Then she whispered something indicating the youth to continue his work. So they tested different positions until she underwent a second climax. Then the woman stretched on the bed, opened her legs and instructed:

"Now penetrate me, I want to feel you inside me."

During the rest of the morning they copulated several times and then they lay exhausted side to side completely covered in sweat. Exhaustion finally overcame their resistance and excitement and made them sleep for hours.

Fatima opened her eyes and blinked several times. A slim ray of afternoon sunlight that filtered between cracks of the roller shutter hit her right in the face. She found herself embraced by a young man and what happened quickly came back to her mind.

She got out of bed being careful not to wake the man and entered the bathroom; all her movements were stealthy like a cat. Personal hygiene was meticulously performed and then she showered quickly putting on a robe on the naked body.

Then she returned to the room and sat in a chair facing the bed. Fatima looked at the sleeping man and set out to make a balance of what had happened, which she had postponed to be able to savor it at will. Indeed, the events of that morning were highly rewarding. She had been meditating about a change in her life for some time and was choosing which elements would be part of the new era. The week before when she had seen the boy for the first time entering a room on the same floor with a fat woman in her fifties, she had conceived the idea of including him in her network. Indeed she realized that she needed a stable relationship with a man in her life, and had fancied this particular youngster in the moment she saw him, but until that morning there were many questions about her ability and the wisdom to do so: could she tackle it with success? Would he be interested in a relationship not based on money? Would she be able to handle the situations that eventually presented to her will? Would he be the kind of vigorous lover that she needed? Would she wake up in him the devotion for her that she intended? Would he be a thug, or addict, or a violent sadist? Doubts assaulted her in droves.

Fatima felt very confident in her beauty, her body and the lure that her exotic features exercised in men, as well as in the firmness of her character to carry out her designs. She had almost always achieved the objectives she proposed to herself, but there was always an imponderable element that could fail. This time what she had achieved with the boy- whose name was not yet known and whose voice she had barely heard- exceeded her expectations. Her doubts and fears dissipated, Fatima knew that she could trust her instincts. Her sense of triumph was complete.

She sat down on the bed, stretched a foot and introduced the thumb in the mouth of the sleeping man. He turned on the pillow but one of Fatima's most relevant features was the persistence in her purposes. He finally woke up, looked at his foot opened his mouth and allowed her to introduce the finger. Then the woman smiled but withdrew the foot.

"I am really pleased for your instincts but I just had a shower. In addition, we must retain some fire for tonight. Now I want to ask you some questions and hear your voice."

He sat on the bed and stared at her for the first time; however he remained in silence.

"What's your name?" The woman took the initiative of the conversation.

"Cristian."

"Your accent is not American. Where are you from?"

"Argentina" His answers were always succinct.

"So you're also away from home. How old are you?"

"Twenty-two years."

The woman was doubly pleased by the confirmation of her conquest youth.

"How long have you been in New York?"

"Almost a year."

"And how did you get here?"

The young man blushed slightly.

"I came with... a lady."

"American?"

"No, Venezuelan."

"Was she old enough to be your mother?"

"Yes, just about."

"And tell me, do you have residence in the US? A green card?"

A touch of alarm appeared for the first time in the youngster face.

"Don´t worry, it is not my intention to betray or finger you or harm you in any other way. It was just a question. So go on, answer it."

"No, the fact is that I am only another illegal in this city."

"And how do you make your living?

"I work in a publication supported by the Puerto Rican community. I am a graphic designer by profession."

"And then there are the ladies, of course."

"Of course."

"What is your last name?"

"Colombo. I'm Cristian Colombo."

"Is an Italian surname?

"Yes, in my country they are very frequent."

"Where are you staying now?"

"I rented a small apartment in Brooklyn."

"In a difficult area?"

"You could say so."

"Would you like to know something about me?" Asked the woman.

"Of course."

"But tell me before what you think of me?"

"That you are a very beautiful lady; your accent sounds French.

"Why do you think that I am a lady and not a prostitute?"

"Because of you behavior... lordly."

"And do you really think I look French?

"No, African."

She considered the questions completed, with evident satisfaction on perceptions of the man, and set out to speak.

"My name is Fatima, and I was born and raised in Chad. Do you have any idea where it is?"

"Yes, in Central Africa."

"Right. I was born in one animist village, beleaguered by the wars between Muslims in the North and Christians in the South. These wars have brought massacres and endless suffering." Fatima looked at the man and saw that he was carefully listening.

"I was educated in France for a long period and ten years ago I came to the United States to study, and completed my Master degree in Administration. Since then I have taken care of the interests of the people of my own ethnical background, who live scattered in my village and other neighboring areas. My father is...let´s say, the authority in the entire region."

"Are you a resident in the United States?"

"Yes, since two years ago."

The conversation lasted all afternoon. Fatima was subtly checking the intellectual and cultural level of the young and intimately was quite satisfied with her findings. He was a quick-witted man although at first impression he looked somewhat opaque. Cristian was under the strong magnetism emanating from the woman, who irresistibly drew him in a physical way, had captivated him with his enigmatic and overwhelming personality, and stroked him with her velvety voice. An invisible network hovered around the couple increasing their mutual attraction.

After several hours both dressed up and went down to the restaurant located near the hotel. Fatima wore a very discreet dark set with pants, and for once went unnoticed among the passengers who filled the hotel's crowded lobby.

When they returned to her room they stripped quickly and rested on the bed, the lady placed once again her slim foot at the youngster mouth saying:

"Well, let's go back at the point we were..."

CHAPTER 2

As he did several times a week, Cristian entered the hotel that afternoon. The concierge barely paid attention to him and continued with his work. He was already well known.

Fatima was expecting him dressed with a light *negligee* that highlighted her curves. From the beginning Cristian perceived a slight change in the woman attitude. He had placed a hand on her hip but she smiled and gently moved away. They had been meeting for two months walking around New York, roaming department stores to which the African was very addicted, taking tea in elegant lounges and had dinner together. Upon returning to the hotel, they made love as if it were the first time. The woman always found appropriate positions to achieve mutual satisfaction. Cristian was soon convinced that they were not part of a practiced baggage but instinctive gear that the lady came equipped with. He had already heard about the exuberant sexual ardor of black women and his experience just confirmed it.

Fatima saddened for the scarce apparel Cristian had brought with him had purchased some formal clothing for his outputs and insisted in his trying them. However that day she looked a little distant.

"Something troubles you Zouby? You look concerned."

"Actually I'm not worried, but I do have something important to tell you. Something that you have the right to know."

Cristian remained in an expectant silence.

"I'm pregnant... logically of your child."

The man despite a barely perceptible slight shudder, as it was his custom made a respectful silence until she resumed her speech.

"I can imagine that you must be thinking "you cannot lie down with a black woman without finding out the next day you're going to be a father""

"Not! No! I would never think that of you. What I want to know is what you intend to do; go forward or..."

"Of course I intend to go ahead with the pregnancy. I am 34 years old and it is time to have a son. In addition, I will be honest with you; I have not taken any precaution to prevent pregnancy because ultimately I want to have your son."

"Well, this is flattering." Said Cristian blushed as it was his custom whenever a mention regarding him was made. "Then it is good news."

"It is without doubt good news for me, but I don't want to tie you to a commitment you've not wanted. If you don't want to recognize him as your son I will understand." And she added "You don't even have to stay with me against your will."

"No! In no way I would leave you. Depart from you in this situation would be something that I could never forgive myself." He paused. "And how will you stand in front of your family and your people?

"I became aware of the pregnancy already a couple of days ago. Yesterday I contacted my mother in Chad and told her. She was happy because it will be her first grandchild. My only sister is still young and unmarried. My mother was losing hopes of becoming a grandmother; what for an African is devastating in a country in which women have an average of five children. She is going to lay the groundwork for tell it to my father."

"How do you expect he will react?"

"He hoped to marry me to a tribal chief, that is why I left Chad and came to America. I think that the idea of having a *métis* grandson will disturb him for a couple of days, but then he will rejoice also. I'm his favorite daughter and objectively he needs to have a numerous offspring given his role in the village. His may not be a sterile branch."

"Will he accept a *métis* grandchild as you called him?"

"All the villages in the area are mixed to some extent for some time; ours is the exception. The Arabs and the French have left their mark... and well?

"Well what?"

"Can I count on you as the father of my child?"

"Of course. I already said that I will not leave you. You already are a very important part of my life."

"Well. This will change a lot how things are between us. To begin I invite you to move tomorrow with me. I'm going to ask for a more spacious room at the hotel."

"I have paid my apartment until the end of the fortnight."

"To hell with that! You move out tomorrow. I don't want to be far away from you one more day." Fatima could not tell whether her rage was real or simulated.

Defeated his formal rather than real resistance, Cristian accepted finally to move, but he was still reflective and quiet, so the lady asked.

"What's now in your head?"

"What do you would have done if I had answered that I preferred not to accept the responsibility of being a father?"

"I would have thought of something to make you change your mind."

"Something like what?"

"Persuasion, lust, threats, bribery..."

New silence of Cristian.

"Well, what are you thinking now?" She asked.

"I prefer lust, it suits you best."

"You have not heard my threats yet!"

Fatima dragged him to the bed and removed her negligee. While she lay down next to the man, she whispered some unintelligible words in his ear.

"What you said?"

"It´s our dialect." She replied with a smile. "I said that the hart has finally fallen into my trap."

"And who is the deer?" Asked him playfully. " And what's the trap?

"You are the deer, stupid, and I have the trap between my legs."

"Have you planned all this in advance?" Asked him as they hugged and kissed passionately.

"Meticulously. From the first day I saw you."

"And now you're boasting?"

"Of course. We must celebrate the triumphs."

The man did not answer; Fatima realized that he was thinking.

"Pondering again! What are you thinking now?"

"In what you just said. What kind of threat?

"Oh, no!" "the woman decided to give him a lesson. " In my tribe unfaithful husbands are ritually castrated."

Despite the joke tone a chill traveled the spine of the youngster.

The following day Cristian came into the hotel early. He had warned his employers in the Puerto Rican Barrio House Organ that he was taking a day off for moving. Since it was an informal employment it was feasible to make such arrangements.

The *concierge* of the hotel saw him enter with luggage for the first time, but he had been warned that Cristian was moving to the hotel so that it not surprised him. He greeted him with a friendly gesture; he had already taken sympathy by the scruffy boy who had formed a couple with the distinguished African lady.

"Afterwards give me your name and passport number to write it down in the guestbook."

The new room was much more spacious that the one Fatima had before. Shea was hanging her clothes-very abundant and varied- in the broad closet. As Christian showed up with an old damaged aircraft suitcase equipped with wheels and a backpack for all baggage she whispered.

"This is all you have?" asked "So much the better, so I have more room in the closet. This is your corner." She added pointing to one end of the unit where there were already hanging garments Fatima had bought him and that had stayed at the hotel.

After finishing accommodating all the possessions of both they went to lunch at the small neighboring restaurant. Upon their return both lay on the bed.

"Cristian." said Fatima "Now that we are going to live together we must establish some rules. You will be my man for as long as you want to be and I will not have another man" Cristian listened carefully "And you won't have other women unless I order you otherwise. Gone are the "ladies that you used to accompany". Do you agree?"

Cristian nodded and although the phrase "unless I order you otherwise" was indecipherable he did not make comments in this regard.

They also agreed that the man would keep his work on the Latin publication but that he also would help Fatima in her unofficial representative of her ethnicity role in numerous forums. As he was an illegal immigrant Cristian could only go to sites that had no formal character. The woman began to explain the nature of the work she carried out, and before the boy she displayed a wide range of very varied high responsibility functions that influenced the welfare of many people from Chad residing in New York and other cities in the United States; the activities also included the management of substantial funds to pay for various services.

As his participation in different negotiations unraveled in front of him the scope of Fatima´s actions in favor of Chadian refugees in the United States and residents in Chad, as well as linkages with other African countries a sense of admiration for the capacity of the woman began to grow in Cristian, as well as for the professionalism with which she faced her responsibilities. He could not stop comparing her with the idle, bored and parasitic women that had alternated with since he had left his house.

Fatima used to go out early in the morning and performed her tasks until late in the afternoon so that only at night they got mutually abreast of the day developments.

One day they resolved to go together to the United Nations building despite the irregular situation of Cristian in New York because Fatima had gained confidence in the skill of the boy and wanted to present him to certain African diplomats with whom she was linked in her activities, so that he could replace it when necessary.

They took a taxi in front of the hotel, and immediately Cristian saw something that caught his attention. During the trip he was silent looking repeatedly through the rear window.

Arriving at the U.N. building, he surreptitiously stepped out of the taxi and followed a short distance on foot. Then he clearly saw that the dark blue Dodge which had followed them from the hotel stopped sixty feet further back the taxi from which Fatima was descending. Cristian had already prepared his cell phone for taking pictures and got a half dozen from the back of the Dodge, passing beside the stopped car and from the front. There was no doubt, three black men were travelling in the car, two of them got out and mixed with the crowd, following Fatima in its entry into the UN. Cristian also took clear photographs of them.

Once inside the building he called the lady cell phone, who told him to what office he should go to meet her and her partners.

At the end of the meeting Cristian took the woman by the arm and led her through the halls of the building to make sure that they were not being followed.

As they returned in a cab to the hotel Cristian told the woman his findings, and showed photos of Fatima's persecutors.

"I have no idea who they are, I've never seen them." And after a few moments of silence she added. "As soon as we arrive at the hotel I will be in contact with a man my father knows in New York and whom he fully trusts for security affairs."

"Who is he?"

"His name is Malik. He was born not on Chad but in the Central African Republic. He was a persecuted politician whom my father helped to escape to the US and then protected his family in our village until they could meet with Malik in this city. He would give his life for my father if necessary. I'll ask him to dine with us."

They arrived in the restaurant at 7: 30 p.m. and sat at a discreet table, out of the line of sight of the door and windows.

"Does he know you?" Asked Cristian.

"Yes. We have met a couple of times. No doubt, we will recognize each other."

At that time a formidable looking man entered the local. He was as tall as Cristian but had twice his weight, wide shoulders and lengthy arms, with a round skull and bald head, his skin was as black as Fatima's. The woman made the presentations and explained to Malik the reason for the urgent meeting. The conversation was developed in French and an African *patois* so Cristian understood very little.

"Show me your photos." Malik told the youngster in English, language that they continued talking.

Malik observed meticulously the photos sliding them into the camera screen one after another, after which he said with certainty.

"Princess, I know these people. They are extremely dangerous and responsible for countless refugees' murders. I will take care of them, but it is necessary that you take precautions from now on. I'll call you tonight. Have your luggage prepared."

Fatima and Cristian were already sleeping when her cell phone rang which she had left purposely turned on.

"Madame, I am Malik. I apologize for the hour. The men following you will no longer bother you, but I have consulted with my people and you must immediately leave the hotel because they have already located you. You must say to the concierge that you are living town. In an hour I will be waiting at the lobby and bring you to a safe place."

Fatima and Cristian prepared their luggage at full speed, paid the hotel bills and loomed to the cold New York night. A dark car flashed its lights and approached; Malik was inside and helped loading the bags in the large car trunk.

"Princess, I have already made hotel reservations for both of you. The place to which we are going is safe but you must remain secluded for a couple of days until we ensure ourselves that there is no one lurking around."

The hotel was small, elegant and discreet, located in the Gramercy Park area. They booked in and thanked and bid farewell to Malik. Their room was located on the fifth floor.

"What is this treatment of Princess?" Required Cristian "Is it not somewhat bombastic?"

"No, it's actually the title they give me in my village."

"You belong to the aristocracy among yours?"

"Yes, or is that the nobility only occurs among whites?"

"I did not mean that. I told on the first day that you have a lordly appearance and manners"

Cristian had lit the TV and at that time they were showing New York firefighters extracting from the East River a car with three black men bodies inside. Each of them had received a bullet in the front. The identity and the nationality of those killed were ignored, and was the incident was attributed to a settling of scores between drug gangs.

"It is a dark blue Dodge... waits, it´s **the** dark blue Dodge." Muttered Cristian shocked.

Fatima removed the remote control of his hands and left it on a table.

"Make me love like never before; very slowly and gently. I want your hands and lips all over my body. I want to burn of excitation. And then, only then, you will take me."

Cristian toured the splendid body yet not significantly deformed by the pregnancy. He fully met the requirements made by the woman. Although he was unaware of it, while burning with passion in the mating dance Fatima was leading him to perform with their bodies a dark African ritual celebrating the extermination of their enemies.

CHAPTER 3

For a few days they restricted their movements to the area surrounding Gramercy Park, the neighborhood was quiet and elegant, and its ambience captivated them immediately although they could not enter the square, latticed and with a door for which only residents had key. Malik finally called Fatima.

"Madame, we have controlled the area and it is clear for now. You can cautiously expand your movements but you must avoid all sites where you can be detected. This includes refugee organizations and diplomatic offices, including the UN building.

"And how shall I carry on my activities? There are many people whose safety and well-being depends on them."

"I suggest that you delegated in... your boyfriend as much as possible. As far as we know he has not entered into the radar of our enemies. Anyway, it is important that also he maintains a profile low. We can open the doors of many sites but from now on it will depend on his skill and discretion."

"Well, I will speak with him and then confirm his decision to you."

Fatima had conversed at length with Cristian, and had bluntly explained to him the dangers to which it would be exposed. The young man accepted immediately.

"I think with your state of pregnancy it is also convenient that you may rest a little more."

"Nonsense, just going by the third month. Anyway, I will be working in a small office that we have rented in W4th Avenue, near here. In addition, staying at the hotel I would go crazy. As for you, I think that you should leave your work in the Puerto Rican

27

neighborhood. These new activities are full-time, as you've seen with me."

Then disassociated from the Puerto Rican journal Cristian began to loop through the contacts of Fatima being introduced on numerous occasions by Malik or some of his partners.

He then got in contact generally with informal and loose organizations of Africans from Chad and neighboring countries, but of the same ethnic origin.

The cells in New York gathered funds collected inside and outside USA and channeled them in the form of shipments of food, medicine, equipment and cash to the huge refugee camps that survived in painful form to the wars and ethnic cleansing carried out in the center of Africa. They also dealt with people who arrived in the country from those fields of refugees, mostly women and children. Certain other activities were carried out personally by Fatima with people who interviewed her in her small office. Cristian boasted that it was about weapons although he refrained from asking his girlfriend. For the first time in his life he experienced the feeling of doing something important, whose effects would affect people other than himself. Moreover, that lives were critically dependent on what he did. The obvious satisfaction of Fatima with his work was just a bonus.

The woman was in fact extremely pleased with the performance of the partner she had chosen. The fact that he had made a living on their relationships with older women had originated doubts about the ability of the young person to serve on important things. She was glad that her infatuation with Cristian had not clouded her judgment in terms of his qualities and potential.

As they returned to the hotel and after a shower together they usually went out to visit the peaceful neighborhood, inhabited in different times by artists, writers and intellectuals seeking a haven away from the notoriety but still in the heart of the city of New York. They walked hand in hand by the tree-lined streets, she displaying her incipient tummy, for scandal of some decked up old Lady's who wondered how it was possible that this black woman dared to show her half caste pregnancy, but also the friendly smiles of residents of more liberal spirit. Fatima and Cristian would remember those months in Gramercy Park as an oasis of joy and fullness.

Already winter had descended on the city of New York. Cristian had gone to a dilapidated building in the Bronx located in an area inhabited largely by recent clandestine immigrants, district of violent reputation; the man had reached the place not without some reservations. Young and old persons of Jamaican or African origin watched him with their huge eyes from rickety buildings stairs; small bands of unemployed teenagers looked at him defiant, some of which were certainly under the influence of various substances.

Cristian pulled out his cell phone and called to the site where he was heading to let them know that he was arriving, caution suggested by Malik in the visits of the young white man to dangerous neighborhoods. A few blocks beyond he was about to enter a building that looked abandoned, when from the shadows two figures swooped and tried to immobilize him. Cristian did not see them coming but reacted immediately, applied a kick on the knee of one of the aggressors who gave a cry of pain while trying to deal with the second who however, surpassed him in weight and strength. The young man uttered voices asking for help, but saw that all the characters that were in the portals of houses disappeared inside of them. Finally the attacker knocked him on the ground and saw that the other man had incorporated and approached. Both men were very corpulent, one of them hit him in the face to reduce him and when he fell on the floor the biggest sat on his chest and began to suffocate him. Cristian then fainted. When he just had recovered a spark of lucidity he believed he heard a great noise, as of cans that fell and rolled. The weight on his chest is suddenly lightened and he could glimpse dark figures fighting stubbornly. A light reflected in the glass of a window and one of the solid figures fell in rales. He then heard two shots and someone jogging down the street as well as moans of pain. He felt then that they raised it with care and transported by a staircase, and then everything went out.

Cristian woke up in a bed ramshackle, completely bewildered and lost. He saw a black man who approached and whispered something in French. At that time he felt severe pain in the chest.

"You have crushed ribs and bruises throughout the body." The voice was familiar, and after a few seconds he identified it as Malik´s. Indeed the African came and put his big hand on his shoulder. "Other than that don't have anything serious. You'll be sore several days, even more than now."

"You got away of a good one." He said.

"What happened?" Asked Cristian.

"They tried to kidnap you, perhaps to know the whereabouts of the Princess. You did very well letting us know in advance that you were coming and my friends were waiting. As they noticed that you did not arrive in time they got worried and as they heard noises in the street they realized what was going on and left armed. One of the attackers shot twice without hitting the target but one of our stabbed the other. He will not stand up again.

At that moment they heard coming from the street the siren of several police cars that were coming to the scene of the fight.

"Don't worry". Continued Malik "They will find the body several blocks away, and there will be absolutely no witnesses, all were watching TV and there was no one on the street."

Cristian incorporated with a moan.

"How did you found out?" He asked Malik.

"Ives called me immediately." Malik answered pointing to one of the Africans who were in the room. He also called the doctor." This time he pointed to a fat man who was closing his case. "He had to give several stitches on the face and shoulder, but you will be well. Can you move?"

"I hope I do." Responded Cristian with not much confidence.

"Well, I'll take you personally along with the Princess; we will give several turns to make sure not to follow us. Still I do not know if you were attacked because you are related to the Princess or it was a blow at random. But we must certainly assume the first hypotheses and redouble precautions."

"Four men already killed around me." Added Cristian with affliction

"Fortunately, the dead were bad people."

"Malik, don't tell Fatima that today another man died

"I see that you don't know the Princess; she will celebrate the extinction of our enemies, and although it is not going to scare her can however contribute to convince her to accept the new security measures we are recommending." The mind of the young man suddenly made a U-turn. "Perhaps she will think of celebrating again." Thought excited.

Three days later Malik and another man of stately aspect showed in the lobby of the hotel where they were staying. Fatima knew the man and said ceremoniously to Cristian.

"Let me introduce you to *Monsieur* Daoud. He is the guide of all Chadians abroad. He has much spiritual ascendancy and is a man of peace. He does not speak English. I am sorry but we will talk in our dialect."

Then the three Africans spent some time talking in their language. Malik did not understand certain paragraphs which had to be translated into French for him. Daoud had a deep voice and spoke gently, and his intonation was relieving; no doubt he was a persuasive man.

At the end of the conversation Fatima translated the core of the chat to Cristian.

"Daoud prevents us that a command of murderers, belonging to the Muslim Government of Chad has moved to New York. It is believed that they are trained by a cell of Al-Qaeda active in Sudan and Central Africa. One of its purposes is to hinder the efforts of the non-Islamic ethnic groups to obtain independence. They have already killed several Chadians, Sudanese, Central African and exiles from Mali and Niger. Daoud believes that it is necessary to reduce interpersonal contacts that can expose us. Watching one of us they discover with whom he gets in contact. To avoid their actions our organization in this country will take a cellular structure and we'll fully use our electronic media and social networking contacts.

"And social networks are safe?" Asked Cristian.

"Precisely because they are open to everyone." Replied Malik "The security services and repression forces of Egypt and other countries in the region failed to curb the popular self-organization. Unfortunately in Chad we are not at the technological level of those countries, but we can organize ourselves outside."

"This will allow me to spend more time with you." Cristian whispered in the woman's ear.

"There is another distinct concern that Daoud transmitted us." Replied Fatima "Processes are accelerating in our homeland. As already told you my father only has another daughter younger than I, and he will need support."

"Meaning?"

"Then we must start planning our trip to Chad that is, if you want to come with me."

"To stay there?"

"Yes. At least in my case."

"But in a few months our son will be born."

"The Chadian women usually give birth at much more precarious conditions. My father is a man of resources in Chad. We will be taken care of."

"In addition..." Malik's sentence remained truncated.

"In addition what?" Asked Cristian.

"In addition. Our son, your son, will be the stem of the eldest daughter of my father, the Chief of my people. A true firstborn. Therefore he will be in the direct line of succession.

"Will he not be a *metes*, kind of impure?"

"I already explained to you that miscegenation is very common in the area. And no, no one will consider that your blood is impure. Your son is called high destinations in my homeland."

CHAPTER 4

Fatima and Cristian were walking through Central Park in one of the farthest from your hotel rides which they had carried out. They sat on a bench and took each other hands. The original relationship based almost exclusively on hormones had given way to a much more complex and rich bonding which included a healthy dose of tenderness. The strict restriction to their outings had enabled them to live intimately so that their mutual acquaintance had grown. Also it had reinforced Fatima´s prevailing role based on a certain indecipherable trait of her character equipped with an intense determination, and her superior psychological resources. Moreover, she had found that Cristian was a young, intelligent and lucid man, resilient in the development of his tasks, to whom the obstacles did not discouraged easily. The woman was aware that the youngster had placed her on a pedestal which had its risks and imposed her certain burdens.

"Fatima, what do we do now?"

The woman interpreted that question in a broad sense, referring basically to the future course of their lives. She had in fact been meditating in this regard, and this time seemed timely to share her thoughts.

"I wanted to discuss this issue with you, and I was looking for the right time. It's something that we started talking about a couple of weeks ago."

"Regarding to the role of our son?"

"Yes. I explained that my father is the leader of our ethnic group in Chad; as you have realized already our people are subjected to many pressures and dangers. According to our customs, the leader must be at the same time head of a solid family which ensures leadership in the

35

future. It is there where our son gets into the picture. It ensures a kind of dynastic endurance which my father already despaired of getting. But..."

"But what?

"The stem must be born in our country and in our territory."

"You confirm that you intend to return to Chad?"

"Yes. Two days ago I talked to my mother on the phone; she told my father of our situation and could convince him to accept it."

"That means that the big boss is ready to receive you back?"

"With a condition."

"Which one?

"That we get married. A future boss cannot be a bastard."

Cristian's face changed imperceptibly his expression.

"I see that you don't like the idea." Challenged the woman without showing the high degree of tension she was under.

"No, it is not that. It happens that he had never considered seriously the possibility to marry. This takes me suddenly...."

"The question is would you marry me?" Fatima's voice finally betrayed a hint of anxiety, strange to her temperament.

This time Cristian did not hesitate.

"Yes, of course."

A deep feeling of happiness swept through Fatima body. The man who she had chosen would be finally hers.

"There is another condition: the marriage must be in accordance with our ritual."

"Do not worry, I have no religious preference."

The trip to N'Djamena, capital of Chad took place in several stages. First they from New York to Paris where they stayed for a few days always avoiding any exposure to prying, as Malik had already warned them that the French capital was riddled with agents of all nations and ethnicities of the former French Equatorial Africa, who perhaps would have already been warned by their contacts in New York over the fact that the daughter of a powerful Chadian chief was in motion, and it was easy to foresee that in the possible trip to her country Paris was a scale little less than inevitable.

The ulterior trip by plane led them through the desert of the Sahara, which occupies all of northern Chad, journey in which Cristian could realize the desolation of this vast wasteland, not suitable for human life except in few isolated oasis.

In N'Djamena agents of the father of Fatima were waiting them, which sped up the process of entry to the country and erased its traces in such a way that it could not be tracked by potential hostile elements. Ultimately, those who arrived in N'Djamena were Mr. et Mme Colombo. Even after the precedent in New York Cristian was surprised by the drastic security measures and the means deployed by his future father-in-law people.

They immediately brought them up and loaded their suitcases in an old and ramshackle Citroen van in intent not to draw attention. They traveled in the vehicle through the shrubby plains of the Sahel, intermediate area between the Sahara desert and a little more fertile savannas located in the Southern part of the country. It was a grueling trip, which forced them to drink liquid continuously to avoid the always threatening dehydration, and which Fatima endured stoically the inconvenience pregnancy produced her in these circumstances, particularly because of the continuous jumps of the vehicle tripping over loose stones.

Eventually they began to see the first groves of acacia and other thorny bushes which introduced a note of greenness in the arid landscape. Shortly thereafter appeared the first huts, isolated at the beginning and then forming villages of a certain size.

At one point, Fatima pointed with a certain excitement a human complex in front of them and exclaimed.

"There, that's my village, my true homeland!"

Cristian watched amazed as tears ran down the cheeks of his woman. For the first time Fatima showed in his eyes a sensitive and even vulnerable side. It was a strong experience for the young man to discover the more human side of the woman with whom he had already shared five months and that until that time had been the cold and fearless daughter of a powerful African chief. Instant revelation showed an aspect that had eluded his perception that long.

As they descended from the vehicle a crowd met spontaneously to celebrate the return of the Princess, who so much aid had procured her people from abroad. Children and young people who were not even born when Fatima had gone saluted her with joy and enthusiasm. Fatima replied to the greetings with an upright posture and with a somewhat rigid and invariably smile, while a knot formed in the throat of Cristian by the thrill of the unexpected welcome. He looked at his woman and saw her looking forward with dignity as if she were looking through her subjects, but the strong emotion that Cristian had witnessed an quarter of an hour earlier at the first sight of the village made him think.

"You do not fool me, you are adopting a regal pose but ultimately you are moved to the bone."

The reception of the villagers was warm and enthusiastic and increased the strong emotion Fatima was going through, and surprised Cristian since he knew that they had not seen their Princess for about fifteen years. The young man began to meditate on the intensity of tribal ties, an unexpected feature of reality.

After a while a figure emerged from one of the houses made of bricks and concrete located in front of them. It was an elder woman of magnificent aspect, beautifully dressed with a violet silk outfit covered with small shiny stones, and on whose head wore a hat in the same colors. Cristian, no expert in fashion and even less in African costumes could not less to admire the picture of the person who approached surrounded by a retinue of ladies and children.

"*Maman.*" Moaned Fatima, with her pride completely overtaken by her heart and her face flooded by tears.

The two women hugged each other without being able to articulate a single word for a long time, during which groans and cries were mixed. Cristian and the rest of the bystanders also crossed by the emotions kept a respectful silence.

The matron walked away slightly and told her daughter in French in a tone that was intended to be of reproach.

"And well Fatima in fifteen years out of home have you forgotten your manners? Are not you going to introduce me to this gentleman?"

"*Bien sûr, maman.* Let me introduce my fiancé, *Monsieur* Cristian Colombo." Then she turned to the man." Please meet my mother *Madame* Souady Djalali."

Cristian followed a hunch and took the matriarch hand and slightly leaning kissed it. Although the woman's face did not reveal any emotion he felt she was surprised and pleased.

Then Fatima completed the introduction of her fiancé to the remaining members of the entourage that surrounded Madame Souady Djalali. In the case of younger members, it became expedient that her mother made submissions because they were born after Fatima's departure.

Finally it was turn of the last person of the procession, a young woman adorned simply with a wide deep blue dress that partially covered her head, but exposing a beautiful African face in which highlighted two huge eyes that stood out against the dark skin and her lips that were painted in the same color of the dress. Fatima jumped in her arms and both wept profusely with joy.

"Cristian, *ma soeur* Charfadine. She was only five years old when I left home."

The young man shook the girl's hand trying to hide how much her beauty had affected him.

"Now I am the one who has forgotten manners." Said Souady after a moment. "please Fatima, say goodbye to our neighbors and let´s enter the house. From now on you will have plenty of time to socialize with them."

The Djalali clan members were gathered around a table.

Fatima and her mother were trying to keep the conversation in French -which everyone including Cristian could understand- but the dialect mixed spontaneously making translations necessary.

Souady had already explained that her husband Ousmar Djalali head of the clan and in reality of the entire ethnic group was traveling in the area of Savannas of the South where he had important trading partners. However, upon learning of his daughter's coming he had rushed his return and he would be in the village in a couple of days during which he would have to travel partially by camel. She finally asked.

"And well Monsieur Colombo, where are you from?"

"I am Argentine. I was born in a town of the Province of Santa Fe called Venado Tuerto." Cristian translated the name of the town the best he could and thought that the meaning would be alien to his partners, but in reality it was accepted naturally in a rural environment as the Chadian society.

"Your surname sounds Italian." Souady was orienting the conversation.

"Yes, they are fairly common in Argentina and in Santa Fe in particular."

"And how is it that you speak French?" For the first time Cristian heard Charfadine velvety voice.

"My grandmother was born in France and lived in my parents´ house. She taught me her language when I was a boy, but I have very little practice."

"And what is your profession or job?" Souady resumed the control of the conversation.

"*Maman*!" Rebuked Charfadine "M. Colombo will believe that we are interrogating him." You tell her!" Emphatically asked her sister.

"Oh! Non, non. It is logical that Maman wants to know who I brought home and who is the father of the child in my womb." Answered amused Fatima waiting to see how her boyfriend got away without mentioning his activities in New York when they first met.

"Well. I am a graphic designer..."

After Cristian's presentation the conversation revolved around events of the past, prior to the departure of Fatima to America, which somehow had been a milestone in the family history.

"Actually I'm not surprised to see the groom you have." Said Souady to Fatima, who got prepared for an episode of embarrassment "He looks very much like to that French lieutenant by whom you were fascinated at the age of fifteen. Remember him Nye?" inquired addressing one of the aunts of Fatima and Charfadine.

"Yes, but the truth is that with that uniform he had fascinated all young women in town, and some who were not so young including me!" Replied the loquacious and funny Nye.

The meeting continued for two hours, until Souady ruled that the newcomers would be fatigued and deserved a rest before dinner.

They had accommodated temporarily in one of the bedrooms of the House of Fatima's parents and had just arranged their belongings, while most of the clothes still remained in the suitcases. Fatima was tired by the succession of air and ground travels and leaned on the large bed that had been prepared for them. Cristian was still placing his clothes in a rustic wardrobe, when he observed his fiancé, who had made an intriguing gesture with her finger, Fatima had indicated him to approach, and in her expression the man could read what went through her head. He sat down on the bed and tried to come close to her, but the woman stopped him by placing one foot on his face, keeping him at a distance. His feet were small for the size of the African, and were well formed; Cristian kissed the soles of the feet and she introduced one thumb in his mouth.

"Would you like...?"

"I want to repeat what we did at the hotel in New York on the day that we met, and we have not repeated since then. Without so many stunts by my pregnancy, of course."

He continued his loving exploration with the ankles, calves and knees, Fatima shook emitting small groans that the man knew were caused by passion. Indeed he knew that Fatima would never pose an orgasm or excitement to stimulate her lover, as that would not be in accordance with her demanding character in sex and in anything else.

Arriving at the thighs the groans of Fatima grew in intensity and frequency. After a few moments she sat on the bed, took her man by the shoulder, and laid him flat and then lowered his pants and underwear. Cristian then realized she had already taken out her panties, which confirmed that the whole performance was premeditated, what did not surprise him in the least.

Fatima sat on the erect penis and began moving her hips in a rhythmic and slow manner increasing the penetration but the movement soon turned faster confirming her state of arousal, the pace increased until it became frantic. At that time was heard a noise in the house hallway leading to the bedroom where they were; Fatima quickly changed her position contorting her body in such a way that ended up sitting on his face. Always in a hurry she took several blankets surrounding her and covered the entire body of the man and his own lap. Instantly appeared Souady with her usual and imposing tribal attire.

"Fatima."

"Oui, maman."

Souady continued talking in dialect although jumping as usual from one language to another in the course of their colloquial chats. They talked for a long time while Cristian- who was immersed among blankets and half suffocated by them and by the buttocks of his fiancé-could not follow the conversation. Finally Souady went to the door, but before she said.

"Fatima."

"Oui, Maman."

"Remember that you're heavier because of your pregnancy and let that man who is under you at least breathe."

The matron became closer to the bed and flipped the blankets away, exposing Cristian.

Her mother was one of the few people who were able to make Fatima jump by surprise, since she had believed that the coverage had been effective to disguise the situation.

"Maman, is not what it seems." She managed to say.

Souady, unnerved by the absurd answer of his daughter again resorted to dialect.

"Your father is a warrior; I never had him buried between my buttocks."

"Then you don't know what you've missed."

The mother shook her head and came out with an angry -partly real, partly fake- gesture. Fatima emitted a sonorous laugh while Cristian, quite confused, tried to emerge from his submitted situation.

"Stay where you are. I haven't finished with you yet!" Was the emphatic order received.

Satisfied Fatima's desire the man asked about the dialectal talk with her mother.

"So she caught me in a position that she considers humiliating. She will feel contempt for his future son-in-law!"

"She rather feels envy of her daughter. But don't worry; all she understood of your presentation is that you're Italian."

"...but I never..."

"...and the Italians are known in this part of Africa as men of insatiable and extravagant sexual instincts."

"... insat... extrav... but who of us was...?"

Fatima placed one of his long fingers on the lips of the man silencing him, as she said

"Don't you dare to divulge our couple secrets! Remember always that I am a Princess, so the only possible culprit is you."

Then she kissed him on the mouth and took one of his hands and placed it between her thighs.

"... insatiable. All right, blame the bloody Italians."

CHAPTER 5

From far away they saw the cloud of sand raised by the old Toyota wheels, and numerous villagers who had not tasks to perform gathered around the diffuse road leading South.

When the vehicle arrived several people got out of it looking tired and filthy after their long trip. Among them was a tall white bearded man showing regal attire despite the dust that covered him.

Fatima, who had been warned of the arrival and had gone out of the house approached the newcomer and stood up a few feet away from him. The man watched her from that distance, hesitated a moment and then opened his arms. The young woman threw herself into them and both were confused in a long, silent hug.

Cristian, located to a certain distance could not hear what father and daughter said to each other and waited quietly until she turned and beckoned him to come closer.

The two men shook hands silently. Cristian felt scrutinized by the elder, whose presence was overwhelming but did not let the patriarch intimidate him and returned his steady gaze. If Ousmar Djalali had tried to frighten his future son-in-law he had to recognize that despite his fragile appearance the attempt had failed. If on the contrary had tried to measure his resiliency he had been more successful.

In any case, the tribal chief, who on other occasions had managed to assess at first glance the reliability of a man this time had to postpone his decision.

Fatima made the presentations, and Cristian got to whisper:

"*Enchanté.*"

Ousmar Djalali surrounded her daughter's waist and together they walked towards the house; Cristian followed them a few steps back and could barely perceive that they were speaking in the African dialect.

That morning, Fatima returned to the rooms with her boyfriend and remained silent while she changed her footwear.

"Well." Said expectant Cristian.

"Well, by now you've passed the test, which is not a minor thing.

"But I hardly opened my mouth."

"No need. I already told you that I have always been the favorite of my father, in the absence of a son. The fact that I appeared fifteen years later, pregnant by an alien necessarily would produce rivalry between both of you. I already knew it."

"You could have warned me!

"You already know me; you had to prove yourself with your own resources. And you've endured the first encounter. Although I repeat that the opinion of my father upon you is in formation."

"Fatima, I understand your father's central role in the community and in your life, but I am not going to allow him to determine my actions and behavior, I will continue being myself." Cristian tone had turned tense.

Fatima smiled

"That's what baffles me and at the same time what I like in you, that mixture of apparent helplessness and internal control. I'm glad Ousmar Djalali has clashed against that unpredictable wall, and is now perplexed." She approached the man and kissed him with passion. "Many brave warriors turn submissive and lower their eyes when confronted with my father, but you stay still and defiant."She then stood apart and suddenly remembered.

"By the way he told me that he wants to talk with you before dinner."

"So be it."

At the time of the appointment Cristian approached the living room where Ousmar was waiting for him. On the way he saw the back of a woman dressed in a bright blue robe. As he recognized her his heart began beating rapidly against his will. Unconsciously he quickly stepped up until he was by her side. The woman turned around looking at him and their eyes met briefly, but hers lowered immediately while blush dyed her dark cheeks. Cristian, although also affected could not stop beholding her face, beautiful as only that of a daughter of the desert can be.

"Hi Charfadine." Said in a voice that intended to be firm.

"Alo, Monsieur Cristian." She had regained composure and looked him in the eyes, after which continued her course towards the kitchen.

Ousmar Djalali expected him sitting in a large armchair, since he was with hip pains due to travels in camel and horseback during the previous days. Cristian could perceive a subtle difference in the attitude of the African compared with that of the first meeting. He was also showing his authority but without the aura of contemptuous indifference that the youngster perceived then.

The conversation developed in French and in English when the limitations of the young in the first language required it. The old man led him through a series of issues that necessarily produced varied responses and reactions in Cristian, who soothed as he realized that it was not a hostile interrogation but a skillful exploration about his knowledge, attitudes and ultimately his character.

Djalali was discarding motives of ideological, political and economic interest in his relationship with Fatima, and did so with a mastery of a true leader of men. Cristian realized the true meaning and implications of many of the questions and worried about answering with the greatest possible candor. He had the growing conviction to be performing a test and that he was approving it.

At one time Souady appeared in the door; she waited a few moments to avoid cutting the conversation and perhaps to perceive the tenor thereof, and then with a smile announced dinner.

A month later Fatima and his mother made a mysterious trip to Cairo, from where they returned three days later. An air of satisfaction was perceptible in both women although the cause was not reported immediately.

Cristian asked his girlfriend about the details of the trip, and after some evasive received his answer.

"We went to do a gynecological study and to see the evolution of pregnancy, as the sixth month was fulfilled."

"So?

"The pregnancy is going very well, and it is a creature of good size." Replied enigmatically Fatima.

"Aja, what else?"

"Is a male." Added the woman barely containing her joy.

"Ah! Well, there will be one more Colombo in the world." He said with a smile. "I always wanted that my firstborn to be a male."

"But no, he is not just your firstborn Colombo! Do not you realize the dynastic and political implications this pregnancy has?"

"To hell with dynastic implications!" Replied the angry man "This is in the first place about our family."

"Yes, but not only about our family." Fatima used a conciliatory tone and stroked her boyfriend in the cheek. "Cristian, my people are surrounded by historical enemies; we need to be held together. An assured descent of their leaders is an important agglutinant element for their survival."

"In my country we have precisely the problem of families who wish to perpetuate in power."

"Do not compare completely different cultural traditions. In addition, your country is neither determined by an ethnic group nor surrounded by enemies."

"I do not buy the Savior role of leaders; we have already had enough examples that fatally end in corruption."

Unexpectedly Fatima took his face between her hands and smiled.

"I understand your feelings; don't forget that I've been educated in France and the United States. I understand the Republican ideal. I only ask that you accept that there are other ways in which people can get organized. I'm glad that our son has both genes; so he will be open to traditions and the future simultaneously."

This reflection left boy pondering. Fatima was a wellspring of surprises, even in the political field; her thoughts were always original and personal, never attached to clichés. On the other hand, he had to admire once again the way she had driven him, his values and his emotions. The woman always found fair attitudes to smooth out difficulties and overcome resistance.

"But we must return to the theme of our son." She continued. "His coming will overcome my father's resistance. Now is the time to speak of our marriage."

Again the phrase took Cristian off guard, but this time he had already elaborated the theme. He responded immediately.

"I am ready when you are."

Ousmar Djalali sent a message to Christian inviting him to a meeting in the ceremonial tent of the tribe. Fatima immediately alerted her boyfriend about the implications of the meeting. No doubt the purpose would be to introduce Cristian to the other elders and other dignitaries of the ethnic group and allow these to interrogate the stranger about his background and intentions. It was a rite that was performed with all those who wanted to join some of the clans in general by exogamic weddings.

"And what can they ask me?" Wondered the young man. "What can be of interest to them?"

"I have no idea, because it is a purely male space. I only know the female activities. In addition, even if I knew I would not tell you, because it is also my intention to see how you manage. All, more importantly that what you say is how you behave yourself, especially your self-confidence. I will only say that I totally trust you."

The tent was a spacious circle made of embroidered fabrics, about seventy feet in diameter set in the Northern access of the villa, in a desert area. Its sight emphasized its ritual importance due to its size compared to the huts of the majority of the villagers, and its eye-catching appearance.

Inside there were unfolded carpets and some ample cushions placed directly on the sand. When Cristian entered about fifteen men were already seated, all around Ousmar Djalali. They were elderly men except three warriors who were equipped with curved daggers in their belts. The costumes of all of them were luxurious and colorful. They were drinking coffee in small cups and offered one to the young visitor. Coffee was strong and had sediment at the bottom but its aroma and taste were exquisite.

"Well young man." Ousmar opened the meeting "We have gathered today to meet you." His tone was neutral and did not produce Cristian any particular emotion. "Although you already had a meeting with me, I will repeat some questions because I desire that other attendees have the same information I have."

Before beginning with the questions Ousmar introduced each and every man present at the gathering with their names and titles, of which Cristian understood little and retained less. Anyway the one who was being evaluated was he, that was clear enough. Ousman then he introduced the stranger and made a short introduction on the circumstances of his arrival to the village. A silence followed his words.

One of the elders asked Cristian to tell them about his birthplace, education, experience and means of life. In the course of the meeting, the tension that dominated Cristian at its beginning commenced yielding as he perceived that he was properly answering the questions that were asked him. This was something typical in the young man:

initial uncertainty product of his innate shyness being displaced by progressive self-control as he let his natural intelligence solve one by one all difficulties and snares that were presented to him. Cristian looked with the corner of his eye to Ousmar to check if he looked satisfied, but the face of the African was impenetrable; he realized that Djalali was also tense, since he was being tried at the same time for having brought to the meeting that stranger.

The inside of the tent began to fill with smoke product of burning pipes, so that several of the men exhibited fans.

One of the young men with a warrior-like appearance who had remained silent until then suddenly asked.

"Do you have any military training? Are you familiar handling weapons? Have you ever been in combat?"

Cristian reminded Fatima's phrase in relation with enemies lurking around the tribe, and readily realized the importance of the issue. So he opted to reply with total sincerity.

"I have no experience whatsoever in combat. Military service was abolished in my country many years ago and we have not had wars. I have only participated in fisticuffs quarrels when I was a boy."

He felt that the response had been appropriate for some assents of the elderly.

Thereafter, the meeting became more social and not so focused on the figure of Cristian. The men began to withdraw from the store and talking on the outside under the Sun.

The young man waited until Ousmar stood up and followed him silently into the house.

The next day Fatima returned from a short trip to some relative's house and faced her boyfriend.

"I have news on the outcome of yesterday's meeting."

"Did your father tell you something?"

"It is not how the thing works here. My mother drew it out form my father and I drew it from her."

"Everything is structured here." Cristian added with impatience. "Well, ultimately, how was it?"

"You made a good impression because you spoke with sincerity and the most important thing for them was to determine if you have a hidden agenda. Competencies that they assign you with respect to work honestly are acceptable. The loose point is, as you supposed your lack of military preparation, in a contentious environment. It is not acceptable in the husband of a Princess. You'll be very close to the tribe center of power."

"Then they reject me?"

"They are much wiser than that. They will correct the fault."....

"How is that?"

"Giving you a military training course."

"Do they have a course?"

"What they do have is a coach. Actually he is the military leader of the ethnicity: Haroun. He is the warrior who questioned you about your military skills."

"He has a fearsome appearance, with his hand always on the scimitar."

"He is effective in what he does. But I must warn you of something."

"What about."

"Haroun was the man who wanted to marry me when I left Chad."

"In other words I'm going to put my neck in the hands of a jealous rival?"

Fatima laughed loudly and as she did regularly expelled the state of tension out of the scene.

"No, no. That was a long time ago. Now he has married well and has his family. In fact I don't know if he has more than one wife so I'm glad I ran away from him fifteen years ago." And then added with roguery. "You should nevertheless take care of your throat. Who knows what will be his attitude towards the man who got his old love pregnant?

The relationship with Haroun was good from the beginning. He didn't make any mention of the past, and focused on testing Cristian combat skills. He made him practice something of close range fighting with the bare hands and knives. Then he continued with a basic training in weapons, beginning with old Tuareg carbines up to some more modern rifles. At one point Haroun told him.

"I see that you learn quickly and have good natural aim. My biggest question is about your attitude when you have to aim to kill or cut a gorge."

"I wonder if that time will ever come."

"In our country and your future position is question is not if but when." Replied somberly Haroun.

Several weeks after Cristian had started his military training, Fatima asked for his relationship with Haroun.

"As you can see, I still have my neck in a piece, and I think that unpredictably we have certain sympathy for each other. He is some twenty years my senior and treats me as a nephew or something. As military adviser is certainly efficient, the clan is in good hands.

CHAPTER 6

Haroun was waiting for him at the North exit of the village, i.e. oriented towards the Sahel semi-desert area. Bedouin wearing a long tunic accompanied them with three Saharan camels.

"Hello Haroun." Greeted Cristian intrigued for certain changes he had perceived. "What do we have today?"

"We will suspend for a day your training with weapons, taking advantage of the presence here of my friend Hassan." Haroun made a gesture towards the cameleer, who smiled showing his toothless mouth "Hassan will lend us two of his beasts for the day."

After the difficult ascent to the camel Cristian and Haroun rode in silence, while the young man was trying to balance his weight on the animal and made a vain effort to guide it. After a while he desisted convinced that the beast was limited to follow the camel rode by Haroun.

Only after they had traveled about one mile Haroun broke the silence, talking to the young man from one camel to the other.

"I know Hassan since I was a kid, he taught me everything there is on camels and the desert."

"And who is Hassan?" Asked Cristian. "A desert guide or something like that?

"Not exactly. He is a former caravan robber, who was in activity until in a fight with the French Foreign Legion in what's now the Central African Republic he was seriously injured. He is currently dedicated to smuggling and trafficking in persons."

"I see. A pillar of the community."

"He knows the Sahara and this intermediate area like few others. If you were looking for water in the desert you would want to be with him."

A new period of silence while the camels raffled a rocky area that offered some difficulties.

"One of my wives has heard that you're going to marry Fatima, and the child she is carrying is a male."

"So it is."

"I congratulate you, but something inside me would have wanted that that child was mine." He looked to Cristian and laughed. "Don't worry, that is a very old story. Ousmar Djalali should be exultant, although I do not expect he will exteriorize it. His first grandchild! Fatima must have explained you the political importance of the news."

"Yes, although I do not share your dynastic ramblings.

New laughter of Haroun.

"Make sure Ousmar never hears you saying that." He said very seriously however.

Cristian had already realized for some time that Haroun was not a simple warrior but an intelligent man, broad minded like few others in the village and was glad of having him a friend and advisor. He and Fatima were the only ones with whom he dared to speak with sincerity.

"Don't worry, will do it."

After another short stretch Haroun changed the subject.

"Did Fatima speak with you about our customs and traditions for weddings?"

"No, is there something I should know?"

"About the rite I am the wrong man to explain it to you, but there is one issue that I want you to know. It's what you would call the dowry. Tradition calls for the family of the bridegroom, or the same boyfriend, to make a gift to the bride's family." In fact her father."

"You mean something symbolic?"

"Nooo! Something very concrete, usually cattle and in direct relation to the value of the bride, which in the case of Fatima is very high. We are talking about cows, horses or camels."

"As you can imagine, I am not in a position to give a hen. And without this requirement the wedding cannot be performed?"

"Usually not. But don't worry, that's why I bring this subject up."

"And why should I not worry?"

"Because I'm going to give you the dowry that you are going to give to Ousmar."

"I cannot accept that! It would be abusing of your generosity. You already are doing enough for me filling my voids in the military field."

"No problem, I come from one of the richest families of our tribe. This will not affect me financially. In addition, I am already doing an investment in you."

Cristian meditated in silence for a while. He had already seen gestures of generosity among the people of the desert but this exceeded his expectation.

"I am very thankful Haroun. I hope someday I will return you the value of the dowry."

"In no way. A favor is returned with another, not with cash."

They followed in silence. The young man was immersed in deep meditation, product of new life experiences to which he was exposed to every day. It suddenly appeared a thought that had a long incubating inside, and that still had a diffuse way. Cristian had a self-examination capacity unusual in people of his age, which helped him to make clear his feelings to himself. Contact with the village of his bride was rewarding to him and he could recognize that a sense of belonging was developing in him. Despite the different valuations on a myriad of topics such as the role of women, the peace, the independence of each individual with respect to their ethnicity and so many others his admiration for the courage, hospitality, dignity, generosity and sense of availability had seized his heart. Haroun's offer had touched him, and was incompatible with the materialistic, cold and calculating society that Cristian came from and to which he had adapted to the point of having lived of women. A cold current of embarrassment ran through his back.

The wedding began as a private act between the families of both parties. In the case of Fatima the present were her parents, Charfadine, her uncles and cousins, including a score of people, all richly dressed in costumes and multicolored tunics of a remarkable visual richness; the Djalalis were wealthy and had the necessity of exhibiting their wealth at that special event, primarily by the political relevance of Ousmar in the village and beyond. In the absence of the Cristian's genetic family only Haroun was accompanying him, dressed in his warrior finery. The groom wore all that he owned in accordance with traditions. Fatima was veiled and hidden at the beginning of the ceremony as required by the rite. The first phase was the delivery of the dowry from the groom's family to that of the bride, which Haroun materialized in the form of fifty excellent cows which were inspected one by one by Ousmar and one of his brothers. As the protocol demanded Ousmar showed not very satisfied but his brother finally convinced him of the quality of the gift. The dowry was therefore adopted, so the wedding previous requirement was fulfilled.

Then arose an animist shaman dressed with bundles of straw and with his face painted with ritual signs, who made several spells in an ancient dialect, asking the great universal spirit by the long life of the intending spouses and the fertility of the couple and their flocks. Just at that time the bride appeared and was unveiled by her father. Fatima could not hide the intense emotion that was upon her. She was dressed in a white tunic with gold appliqué, which quite conceal the pregnancy.

By consecutive three times the shaman asked if she agreed to her marriage and three times she replied affirmatively. Then Haroun gave Cristian a ring that the later placed on Fatima's finger ring. The wedding had taken place, Fatima and Cristian were spouses.

In fact, the wedding itself was rather a process than an act. Three days lasted the celebrations, in the course of which practically all members of the ethnic group, even the very old and those who resided in very distant villages, were presented to bless the couple, bring their opulent or modest gifts and greet the tribal chief and his wife. The wedding not only met its social and family role, but it was an important political act, which welded the union of the ethnicity and the links between its members. Old local feuds were buried and the community spirit reinforced. Ousmar Djalali and his wife were radiant. An aspiration long delayed by the prolonged absence of their eldest daughter had been fulfilled in the brightest possible way.

The echoes of the wedding lasted for several weeks, in which even families from remote villages that had not reached the ceremony for various reasons visited them.

In the meantime, Fatima and her husband had moved to a small house on in the extreme south the periphery of the village, bordering a few groves of acacia and other trees. The housing consisted of three rooms, the largest which served as living room and dining room. A couple of women of the tribe went daily to clean and cook since Fatima was quite limited in her movements due to the pregnancy.

Three times a week Haroun and Cristian met to continue with the training, which had in fact become an exercise for both. One day they had interned more than usual in the desert area located north of the town. They were exercising the close range fight techniques where usually Cristian received a good thrashing, when he realized that Haroun had stopped suddenly focusing his view on the Northern horizon. He followed his gaze and there, clearly cut above a dune located a good distance distinguished the silhouettes of three riders who in turn were watching them. Their robes waved with the wind and on their backs they could see the barrels of their rifles. The scene suggested nothing good and a warning light appeared in Cristian's mind, particularly given the grim frown from his partner.

Cristian cautiously approached the warrior and asked:

"What Haroun? Who do you think they are?"

"They are members of the Goran ethnic group who took over the country a generation ago and covered it with blood. They are Muslims and Arab allies; Although they themselves are of mixed blood they believe that blacks are only beasts of burden. They had never come as far south. I think that they are just explorers, but these men are bad news anyway."

The mood of the two men changed radically due to the omens the riders produced.

"Do you prefer to retire?" Asked Cristian.

"On the contrary. Let´s continue the fight drills, so they realize what they are going to find."

During the way back Haroun was absorbed in his thoughts and the young man respected his silence. When they approached the village the African said.

"Do not talk with anyone about this. I will communicate it to Ousmar in person. He will decide what to do."

The next day one of the servants of the Djalali family approached the house of the couple and communicated Cristian that in the evening there would be a meeting in the ceremonial tent, without specifying the reason.

"I'm surprised this meeting off agenda" Said Fatima "Do you have an idea on what it is about?"

Cristian was cautious to answer but at the insistence of women responded.

"I have I Haroun committed not to reveal this to anybody but your father, and I ask you to respect my commitment."

Fatima, good *connoisseur* of male codes did not insist thinking that in the long run she would learn what happened.

The tent was full of the hierarchs of the tribe when Cristian arrived, who could sit on the ground, on one of the carpets in the fourth row of the audience.

A strong buzz and the tobacco smoke filled the tent, and the prevailing climate was of concern. At a time Ousmar asked for silence and the voices stopped. The Chief explained that news had arrived, and although they were not worrying they still required the attention of attendees. Then Haroun started talking and although Cristian could follow with difficulty his speech in dialect, he understood that the warrior was narrating the display of the Saharans tribesmen in the desert. Then several characters, warriors and merchants, told their experiences of encounters, so far bloodless with Arabs and members of the tribe Goran in places where previously they were not seen, at least in the last decade.

Once concluded the testimonies, the attendees turned to stay silent waiting to hear the words of the Chief of the tribe. Ousmar cleared his throat and began to outline the strategy that they would carry on. Haroun explained to Cristian the contents of the ruling once the meeting was over.

Strong points with heavily armed permanent sentinels were to be established in the North access to the village. Patrols on horseback and camel were to delve in the Sahel to give the alarm in case of movements of potentially hostile troops. All available weapons would be seized, its operation would be controlled and they would be assigned to men in a position to make use of them; all young people would be subjected to a training military of the type that Haroun had performed with Cristian. Emissaries would come into contact with all the allied heads of villages to agree a strategy of mutual collaboration in case of attacks, and finally, spies were to be introduced in neighboring countries to monitor the political and military situation in each one of them and explore the escape routes for the population if the security situation continued worsening. Thus, Sudan, Niger, Nigeria, Cameroon and the Central

African Republic would be evaluated according to the guarantees that they would offer in case of an exodus towards each one of them. Each responsibility was assigned to a man of trust of the tribe. Haroun would be the coordinator of the patrols in the northern border, and Cristian was incorporated into his contingent that would be guarding the hottest spot, where the threats were likely to come from. The youngster asked his friend what would be the role of Ousmar, and the diffuse response he received suggested that first he would travel with unknown destination to make contact with the French, usually last resort guarantors of the animistic tribes against the warlords of the North.

The young man admired the wisdom and leadership of his father-in-law and the respect that he inspired to his followers, and for the first time admitted that a leader was necessary in extreme situations.

Cristian felt free to tell the news to his wife.

"I brought you to this country and almost immediately you're wrapped in a war that is not yours." Fatima expressed with regret.

"It's mine if my family is involved."

"But it is not your people."

"My people are where my wife and my son."

The woman was stunned by the response. Cristian had not shared with her or with anyone the internal evolution he was undergoing and the identification with the members of the ethnicity of his wife, and in fact he himself was surprised for expressing it so clearly.

"However." Added the young man. "I would prefer that you were evacuated as soon as possible. I want to get you and our child safe from any danger."

"That's impossible." Answered Fatima. "My son is the future of this tribe and it must be born among them. He cannot be a fugitive since before birth. At least not by something that, for now, is only a diffuse menace. In any case, we will leave this decision in the hands of my father."

"You have to understand that I am the ultimate responsible for my family, and I will not delegate fundamental decisions in your father or anyone else."

He made a stop to emphasize the words he had said and that had struck significantly Fatima.

"Well." Continued then Cristian. "At the very least we will delineate a contingency plan just in case the situation gets worse.

CHAPTER 7

TWO MONTHS PASSED BY, with moments of tension by alarming news that arrived and were then belied by the facts but allowed to maintain and monitor the degree of alert necessary for the safety of the village.

The gestation period of the son of Fatima and Cristian was completed, and the baby was born normally on May 15 at the start of the rainy season due to the inter-tropical convergence zone, which normally occurs in the area, although sometimes it fails producing droughts of tremendous consequences. In that year it did not fail and rain fell at times torrentially.

A French doctor and his team were mobilized from N'Djamena, the capital of Chad, to be available and assist in the delivery if necessary, but to their relief there was no need of his help and the birth was attended by midwives of the tribe according to traditional methods. This was conceptualized as of good omen by the family Djalali, and increased the satisfaction of Ousmar and Souady as grandparents.

"The birth of a successor is also news that unites us when we need it most." Greeted Ousmar to Fatima.

The baby was named Hubert, French name but relatively usual in Chad, and acceptable since his father was a foreigner.

In a moment in which the mother had been separated from him Cristian approached his son´s cradle and observed him in silence. His skin was noticeably lighter than Fatima´s, hair was not visible yet and the eyes had a watery shade that did not yet reflect their future color. Although Cristian loved his wife surprised himself wishing that the baby had some of his traits. He tinkered by placing a finger in the small hand and allowed the baby to instinctively hold it tight. He had the intuition that was been observed and when he turned back saw Fatima looking at him from up close with a smile.

"Very tender." She said. "This is the first gesture you have with Hubert."

"Because it is the first time that I am alone with him."

"And you cannot do it if someone is watching you?"

"I'll have to get used to this parenting business."

Fatima passed a hand through his hair and her smile became provocative.

"Not only the baby needs your touch."

Cristian knew already his wife and the way she used to express her desires without false modesty.

"I know. It has been a long abstinence also for me." He said, introducing one hand under her robe.

She dragged him to the bed. She was wearing a very light negligee and friction with the outline of her body excited her husband. Cristian lifted her from the ground and placed her on the bed. They merged into a long kiss on the mouth, and then he began to kiss and caress her long neck and breast.

"I see you have not changed your preferences." Said he.

"Shut your mouth and place it where already you know." Was the terse response.

No doubt Fatima had an excitation accumulated for a long time and was insatiable. After a receiving oral sex for a while, she turned on her back and asked her husband.

"Now penetrate me and stay within me until I tell you."

After sex they remained exhausted lying side by side for a while. Fatima soon heard his man snoring and got out of bed. On the way to the bathroom she looked toward the exit and was startled to see a sitting figure there.

"For how long have you been there?" Asked her mother with a tone of anger.

"Long enough." Replied Souady with rogue tone.

"Is it possible that I cannot have relations with my husband without finding you snooping?" The anger was increasing. "You always enter on the sly."

"Dear, I came to visit you and not on the sly. I even stumbled upon a chair and made a loud noise. What happens is that you were twisted in a bundle and did not hear it."

"Did you like our show in your honor? The private function especially for you? At least you could have coughed to warn us."

"In no way. I did not want to distract you. You know I expect from you a grandchild every year and that is precisely the way to achieve them."

"Well." Said Fatima somewhat calmer "let's go out of the house to talk. I don't want Cristian to wake up and realize that we have been doing a little number. Let's save him an embarrassment by a sneaky mother-in-law."

They left the room while Souady went on shamelessly.

"Looks ardent the Italian. Well, they have that reputation. And still lets you sit in his face."

They suddenly heard the baby crying. Fatima left his mother alone and quickly entered the house; passing along the bedroom he saw that her husband was rising entirely naked.

"Ah! *Mon cher*, dress up because my mother is arriving."

"Oh! And where is she?" Asked Cristian flushed.

"Don't worry, she has not yet entered.

The hot July day was forcing them to drink from their water bottles permanently. Haroun had chosen a path towards the Northwest to make daily patrols. Two other men followed them away. Their camels were advancing silently by the sands and had not changed a word in the last half hour.

"Haroun, have been there any news about the marauders in the North, Goran or whatever they are called?"

"Unfortunately yes. We did not want to spread the word not to alarm the villagers, but we have strengthened our precautions." The warrior reported in a low voice. "Three days ago a patrol surprised four riders in a canyon. There was a hard confrontation and three of them fell dead, while the fourth escaped. We lost Habibi, one of the men in charge, coming from one village to the South. Ousmar has a date with a French delegate in the capital in a couple of days. He will ask them to have a contingent of rapid deployment prepared and to give us more modern weapons. Many of our men are armed with rifles one century old and are low on bullets."

"Haroun, I would like to devise a contingency plan to be able to evacuate Fatima and Hubert in case of attack. What escape route would you recommend me?"

"A retreat to the port of Douala in Cameroon. You never know if there may be a massacre like the one in Darfur, and it may be necessary to travel abroad to put distance on this continent. Do you have relatives in your country?"

"Yes. My parents and two siblings with their families. They have a farm, a medium-sized farm."

"What is medium size for you?

"Four hundred acres."

"And would they receive you back in case of need?"

"Yes, I can go back any time and I would be received with joy."

"And you can return to your country or have something pending?"

"I am completely free to return. I left it only for the sake of adventure."

"Do you keep contact with your family?"

"I write every now and then. In New York I had a weekly online contact, but here I have no connection."

"Do they know that you've married?"

"Yes and that we were expecting a child. From there on I didn't give any more details."

"As a military strategy." Said Haroun half-jokingly "I suggest that you prepare a rearguard retreat at your parents. Only your wife and your father-in-law should be informed. As for the rest don't let know for now." Added enigmatically.

Two days later Fatima told Cristian that she was traveling with Hubert to N'Djamena to pay visits to the pediatrician and the gynecologist. She was to join her parents in their trip.

"My father goes on a semi-official visit." She added. "But I have no further information."

Cristian hid the information available to him, but answered.

"I'm going to write several letters to my family in Argentina and send them with some photos of yourself and Hubert. I ask you to send them by mail once you are in N'Djamena.

"Yes. I will do it gladly. Finally you think about them! As for you, you can move temporarily to my parent's house, so some workers can come here to carry out repairs which were pending when we moved."

When Fatima went with his parents to the capital, Cristian walked the distance between the two houses, carrying in his backpack all necessary for a three days stay at his in-laws home. He was received by the servants, who drove him to the guest-room Fatima and he had already occupied when newly arrived at the village. He then left to meet Haroun for their usual patrol, and four hours later returned to the house.

Just after taking a shower and getting dressed he was looking what to do in a house that was not his own and wandered through the long external Gallery when he suddenly crossed with Charfadine. Blush rose to his cheeks despite his attempts to control his emotions. This time it was the girl who took the initiative to initiate a conversation.

"Hello Cristian, are you well?"

"Yes, very well. We haven't seen in a long time." His festive tone reflected his state of mind.

"Twenty days." Replied the young woman with unusual precision. "You've been absent in patrols and were not at home on the two times I went to visit my nephew."

"Ah! Yes. Hubert." Cristian responded somewhat absent-minded. Charfadine raised an eyebrow a little surprised.

"Forgive me." Continued Cristian "It is the first time that I see you with your head uncovered."

Indeed, the women wore all her hair combed in thin braids leaving her broad face exposed. The face was exquisite and Cristian look sunk in her large almond-shaped eyes. When he recovered self-control he noticed an enigmatic smile outlined at Charfadine's lips.

The two youngsters walked along the groves behind the house as if they unconsciously wanted to evade third parties eyes. Both felt lighthearted and failed to notice the passage of time.

"Tell me. How is your country?" She asked." I don't remember its name, but I know that it is not Italy as the others say."

"Argentina. It is a huge country."

"Larger than Chad?"

"Yes, I suppose it is quite larger. It has..."

The talk went on for more than one hour, in which the girl satisfied her curiosity about the birthplace and the adventures of his brother-in-law although carefully filtered by him.

At one point she said.

"We must return, it is getting late and I don't want the people at home to worry for me."

Two days Fatima returned from N'Djamena along with her parents. She looked radiant.

"Both Hubert and I are very well." Said answering Cristian's question.

"The child has grown and gained weight satisfactorily. But before we continue the conversation let me take care of lunch. I have to tell you important things and we will do so after eating."

After lunch both spouses sat in the living room while taking a concoction of herbs of the desert. Fatima started talking.

"My father is very concerned about the political situation and our security; I am referring to the whole village." She paused "He had an interview with the consul and the *attaché militaire* of France in N'Djamena. I think that he has requested military support in the event of aggression of the Muslim tribes of the North." She looked at Cristian and noticed that she had failed to impress him. "Is it you do not care about us?"

"Of course that it is not so. What happens is that Haroun had put me abreast on the topic in a general way."

"My father insisted I consider the possibility of leaving Chad if the situation becomes very complicated. In addition to the military theme we have managed to renew my passport and French visa, as well as documentation for Hubert. This is in accordance with your concern in recent days. Is your Passport valid?"

"Yes. Have you finished?" As Fatima answered affirmatively he added. "Now listen to me, I have to tell you about the rest of my talk with Haroun."

When he finished his talk, Fatima recalled.

"Ah! My father told me that he wants to talk to you this evening. I think that it may be related to these topics."

Cristian came to his in-laws house and a servant lead the way and made him sit in the room. Ousmar appeared almost immediately.

"Thank you for coming. We should have had this talk long before and I am to blame for the delay." He continued without waiting for any answer. "Now you are a full member of this family and our clan, and there are things you need to know, because the future of one and the other depends on them."

As it was his custom, was a moment of silence to emphasize what was to follow.

"Chad borders as well as the frontiers of almost all its neighbors are artificial; they come from the administrative divisions in the former French Equatorial Africa. They have mixed very different people and with a very troubled past among them under a single Government. That is why since independence and the formation of the Republic our history has been filled with coups, ethnic cleansing and slaughters. Of the more than 200 different ethnic groups the majority belongs to two large racial and religious groups. The Muslim Saharan North, speaking Arabic, and Black peoples of the South, related with the Sudanese, divided into numerous ethnic groups, of animist confession, although many have been Christianized by the French. The southern strip of the country is the most fertile, and is the area where cotton crops are obtained so it formed the basis of the economy of Chad until the appearance of the oil. Anyway, we are in one of the poorest countries in the world and the northern tribes have always wanted to expand into our lands.

Cristian listened his father-in-law clear explanation whilst grew inside him a certain admiration for this man, apparently a chieftain of a remote and primitive tribe, but who revealed as a fine politician well adapted to his environment.

"The French colonial period." Continued Ousmar. "which had created this ethnic monstrosity, got to keep it in an unstable balance, but as I said before, from the independence the rivalries exploded, and now we have to deal with the consequences." Here Ousmar made a prolonged break.

"But it was not only to make you aware of our history and our problems that I called it. I need to discuss with you your role at this stage. The safety of my oldest daughter and my grandchild are in your hands and with them the future of our people."

"Trust me. I have the utmost interest in those people. Besides the succession of your clan they are my wife and my son."

Ousmar was not accustomed to that talk in plain and challenging language, but he always knew how to adapt to new situations. In addition he was glad that his son-in-law was not a prude.

"Well, now listen..."

Ousmar began to outline a contingency plan based in part in his own ideas, and partly in responses that Cristian was giving him. When there were no more questions they finished the meeting.

As the young man left the living room he met Souady who also expressed interest in talking with him.

"It seems that after their return from N'Djamena I became suddenly a very important person." He thought.

"Yes, *Madame*, I'm listening."

"Leave the *Madame* treatment to a side. You are already my son-in law. Call me Souady or *Maman*."

"All right Souady."

"There is an issue theme that my husband has probably not mentioned, but which also affects our family, and you must be aware of." Cristian noticed that she in turn began to talk to him in a colloquial way. "Our village does not constitute an actual ethnic group, but that we are a clan within the Sara ethnicity a, one of the largest in South Chad. Further South of our territory extends that of the Mbaye clan, one of the most powerful of the Sara ethnic group."

"I understand."

"The Mbaye have always had intentions of annexing us so we would lose our independence and we would become something like their vassals."

"So Muslims from the North are not the only danger."

"It's a different kind of danger. But yes, there are permanent conflicts among all ethnic groups in Chad, this has always been so. The novelty is that the son of one of the heads of the Mbaye intends to marry my daughter Charfadine."

Souady made a break and observed the reaction of Cristian. This, much to his regret, had been visibly affected by the news.

"Well, I understand." Finally said with a voice thread. Souady continued

"This would be the first step in a series of dynastic conflicts at the heart of our tribe. The Mbaye will try to move to Fatima off the line of succession by all means. You understand the danger."

"Yes, of course." The young man was obviously tense. "And... what does Charfadine think? Rather, what does she want?"

"She does not you want that suitor at all. I think that she is already in love with a man. As well as my husband must deal with situations of war and male issues, you will understand that it is my duty to take care of these affairs."

Cristian waited a few moments to see if his mother-in-law expanded her explanations and told him what she was expecting of him on the thorny issue she had entrusted to him. At the moment it did not occur and the meeting ended there.

The man, impounded by mixed emotions chose to not return directly to his home, so that he made a wide detour through the forests of acacias to calm the turbulences of his spirit.

CHAPTER 8

Ousmar Djalali had invited his son-in-law to join him in one of his commercial travels in the neighboring villages to the South of their home town. The purpose was to travel about 50 kilometers in the savannah that covers the southern part of Chad. They had about a hundred head of cattle, in general young animals born in the breeding areas of the Centre of the country, bordering the Sahel, and sell them to farmers in grassland areas most suitable for the fattening of the beasts. Five villagers with experience in the herding of cattle accompanied them as well as several pack animals, carrying tents and supplies. Ousmar explained to Cristian that the purpose of including him in the group was that, as well as training in military arts by the conflicting ethnic and political situation in Chad, it was also expedient that the newcomer knew the economic activities that supported the clan. Cattle's breeding was perhaps the main one.

"By the rattle on neglected or even non-existent roads every day it becomes more difficult for me to travel on horseback and even in the old jeep that we have. I need someone who will replace me and you are now the closest male member of the family." He spoke in French and Cristian noticed that also Ousmar was talking colloquially to him, what he had never done before, putting the youngster in the dilemma of how to reply.

"Fatima told me that you come from a rural area?" Inquired Ousmar.

"Yes, it is a grain and agricultural area and to a lesser extent cattle-growing."

"What are the main crops?

"Traditionally corn although it has now been partially replaced by soybean."

"Having cereals and meat you eat soy?"

"No, it is largely exported to China and other countries."

"And is your family dedicated to agriculture?"

"Basically, my parents have a fraction of some 400 acres, a little less in reality."

"Then your father is a rich man."

"No, he is what we call a *chacarero*, i.e., a farmer."

"And the rest of your family?"

"One of my brothers works on the farm with my father. The other is an agronomist and has a trade of agrochemicals and seeds. I also have a sister who is a housewife."

Cristian realized that his father-in-law carried on this interrogation for several reasons. One of them was to know the environment from which his son-in-law came, although imagining it was not easy for an African tribal chief. Another reason was to know to what extent Cristian rural experiences could be useful, either in Chad or in another environment if he were forced to split with his family. The worst fear of a father-in-law is the man that his daughter fell in love with is a good-for-nothing.

At any given time he suddenly changed the subject.

"I think that you've already formed an opinion about the situation in this country."

"Yes, to some extent."

"And would you share it with me?"

"I see a great fragility because of the political and ethnic tensions, in a poor society and a natural environment that provides few resources."

Ousmar smiled. It was a good summary and there was no doubt that the man had come to that conclusion himself.

"Well, remember our chat the other day, particularly the last part."

"Yes Sir."

"What do you think we are doing at this moment with these bulls?"

"You are transforming livestock capital in cash, in case you need to flee the country."

Ousmar, whose horse was a step forward, turned and looked at the young man with a wide smile.

"Well, you are astute, as a good son of peasants."

"I come from a country with not as much violence as Africa but much economic turbulence. Argentines are survivors of recurring crises."

"Not a bad training for difficult and changing circumstances."

He pondered in silence for a while and then said in a low voice.

"Worthy daughter of her father."

"Excuse me, what did you say?" Cristian had been distracted.

"Fatima. She knows how to choose a man."

The young man understood that it was a compliment but preferred not to make any comment.

In their stages in various villages Ousmar exchanged animals and other goods they were carrying by local products in a basically barter economy, with occasional sales in money. Each transaction was arduously discussed by Ousmar with their buyers, in hot discussions that finally concluded in agreements. Cristian saw the merchant skills of his father-in-law, who always managed to close a sale. The cash obtained on a site was never used to buy, and evidently his purpose was to return to the village with only money.

Between two stages Cristian made questions about his father-in-law business model.

"Not everything what you sell is self-produced. Right?" Asked the boy.

"No, my subjects deliver me things for sale, relying on my ability."

"A kind of consignment."

"If you say so."

"My questions are aimed at understanding your business."

"I hope you make them, it is really is our business."

Cristian began to understand tasks Ousmar carried out for its individual subjects and the ones he carried out for the village as a whole, and which were the counterpart of the obedience they owed him. He wondered if it was a feudal relationship or whether it was the nature of the State in its intimate essence.

In the next village Ousmar entered into an Evangelical Church while Cristian was walking in the surrounding area. When they met again for lunch the chief told him that he had gotten teaching support for the small school the community was building in the village.

The days were overwhelming for the long stretches that were needed to carry on their trip, leading the beasts under the strong heat at the end of the rainy season. They started each stage very early before dawn and continued traveling up to one hour before noon; then they were stopped in the village at which they had arrived or otherwise under the trees of a some isolated grove, if possible near some water well and pastures for the animals. They thus arrived at the last village they were planning to visit in their trip southbound. Obeying Ousmar´s orders they then undertook the return by another route. Cristian noticed that Ousmar was recognized and honored everywhere.

Already in the midst of the return trip Ousmar had sold all cattle and other goods they were carrying and had transformed them into cash, including different currencies. He was elated and sang a tribal song while he rode. Cristian was riding by him half asleep, since one of the skills he had acquired was to snooze without falling off the horseback.

The shot spooked the horses, some of which tried to run away terrified in any direction. Cristian awaked suddenly completely disoriented and looked to her around. Ousmar was grabbing his left arm covered in blood, while trying to control his horse. Several shots whistled among them. Yussuf, one of the horsemen drew a long carbine from his chair while the other carriers sought to hide away behind the trees of a grove. Without thinking, Cristian took the flanges of his father-in-law horse and drove it gallop after his, while Ousmar was juggling to be mounted with his wounded arm. They soon came to some tall trees, behind which they hid. Yusuff was already on foot hiding behind one tree and Cristian saw that he pointed his rifle in a direction. He followed it with his eyes and distinguished five figures on horseback that precipitated upon them. The young man pointed his finger indicating Ousmar the direction of the danger, a gesture that was immediately understood. The tribal chief took a gun in his hand, and his and old Yusuff's gun sounded simultaneously. Two of the figures rolled along the ground; one of them stood up and rode behind one of his companions, while the other was lying on the ground. Cristian invaded by a wave of adrenaline unknown to him until that moment pulled out the rifle that had been on his horse chair and made three shots in succession towards the attackers. Another man fell on the ground as his horse suddenly freed of its load fled terrified. The surviving attackers opened fire without greater consequences, and in sight of the disastrous outcome chose to flight, three men in two horses. One of the carriers still mounted on his horse made gesture followed them but Ousmar dissuaded him with a scream.

"Let's us stay us together." He ordered. "We do not know if they will return with reinforcements."

At that time, they saw a body lying on the grass under one of the trees behind them.

"Oh! No" Cried anguished Ousmar." Mahamat."

They dismounted and approached the wounded comrade. Yusuff already had preceded them and was kneeling next to the fallen. He looked at Ousmar and shook his head in gesture of negation.

"Nooo! I know him since he was born, I know his wife and their three children." The gesture of despair of the chief was heartbreaking; the carriers turned their heads down in silence. Cristian took his father-in-law's arm in an attempt to comfort him, until he regained his control.

Yusuff had extracted an unsuspected dagger from within his clothes and silently approached the bodies of fallen attackers. As he plunged the dagger into their breasts Cristian saw with horror that the body of one of the attackers-still alive- revolved in agony.

They conditioned Mahamat´s body as they could on his horseback. Yusuff made an emergency bandage on the arm of his boss who was still bleeding in profusion. Ousmar looked him in the eyes, and the muleteer whispered referring the attackers.

"Saharan. I cannot know who they are, militia or just bandits."

They rode away from the site of the battle devastated and in complete silence. The bodies of two fallen aggressors were to the hyenas.

After two hours of march Ousmar broke his silence and turned to his son-in-law.

"You have been brave and determined; no doubt you have saved my life."

Then he looked to the carriers and said in a loud voice.

"All the gain that I've got in this ill-fated trip will be for Mahamat´s widow and her children."

"Also mine." Added Yusuff and thus each of the rest of the men.

That night they arrived at the village. No doubt the news about what happened had preceded them. All the inhabitants were at the southern entrance of the village. The scenes of mourning for Mahamat were heartbreaking particularly for Cristian, not accustomed to such circumstances.

The chief family had gathered in front of their house. Souady barely could hold back the tears, Charfadine had her face covered by a veil and only showed her reddened eyes, who alternately watched Cristian and his father.

Yusuff helped Ousmar to dismount with an unexpected delicacy in a man so rough.

Fatima arrived at the time the men were already walking towards the houses. Wordless she stroked her husband's head in a gesture full of tenderness.

"I remember when I was a child my father and his men brought my uncle on horsebacks after a clash in the desert. It was one of the reasons why I went away at the time."

"But you returned." Answered Cristian.

"I came back, yes. You cannot escape your destiny."

"It is a fatalistic vision."

"The desert generates fatalistic creatures." They had entered their home and taken a seat, and then she placed Cristian head on her shoulder. "Rest here, my love."

Cristian could not overcome his despondency; the scenes of violence and bloodshed did not leave his mind. The fact of having wounded a man who ended up dead was a very strong experience. He lay in bed and was in a state of stupor by hours.

That night broke a strong storm, one of the last in the inter-tropical convergence zone during that year after which the temperature fell sharply. Fatima passed by the bedroom and saw her husband in bed, still asleep by the great fatigue of the previous fortnight, but prey to intense agitation, undoubtedly a nightmare. The woman went to nurse her child, and then slept with Cristian and hugged him strongly. Despite the cold night he was drenched in sweat. She stroked his head and began to sing an old song learned of his grandmother in a very low voice. The sleeping man began to compose in the tender breast of his wife. Fatima, like all African women for generations, knew well what their offspring needed and gave it them tenderly.

The next day Haroun showed up in Fatima's house. In an unexpected gesture the grim warrior tightened Christian in his arms.

"You've acted with bravery and autonomy." And with a slightly bitter smile added. "My shooting lessons have not been in vain." And added winking an eye "Though out of three shots you've only achieved one."

"Haroun." Replied the young. "What is the meaning of what happened?"

"That our prevention and efforts have not been without reason, and that the danger is closer than we think. These men got considerably further South of our village, it is an alarm signal."

"I feel that a glass has been broken in my life. Not only because of the risk situation we went through but because I had to shoot a man, who is now dead."

"Welcome to Central Africa, Cristian. In fact, you are just arriving now."

CHAPTER 9

On the day following Cristian was dressing up to visit his father-in-law who was recovering from his wound, apparently with a good evolution after receiving professional medical attention. Cristian´s energies had been replenished after sleeping fourteen hours. Fatima had risen early and left the house to the same destination.

As soon as he arrived the young man met Charfadine who despite her usual timidity approached him and placed her hand on Cristian´s arm although she withdrew it immediately as she became conscious of her spontaneous gesture. Her face showed anxiety.

"How are you? Have you been injured?" Her voice inflection was equally tense.

Cristian felt a sudden impulse and in turn retained tightly the girl´s little hand between his own. He swallowed, tried to control his emotions and answered in a not very firm voice.

"Do not worry Charfadine about me. I am fine."

"It has been a horrible experience for you." She said.

"Yes, but I've been able to get away uninjured from it." Both looked at the other´s eyes holding the glance for the first time. Cristian guilt was intense, but could not overcome his impulse. After a few intense moments he let go the woman hand and said awkwardly.

"I came to see your father. I know that Fatima has already arrived."

Charfadine also reconvened her attitude and answered.

"Yes, I won´t retain you anymore. Come in!

Both youths were completely confused by the trick feelings had played them, on the one hand by being under the rule of drives which were unfair for Fatima, but on the other hand with a certain joy of knowing that their feelings were shared. Definitely they could not nor want to delete what had happened with them at that time.

The doctor had withdrawn a few minutes earlier and Ousmar was sitting on his bed, accompanied by Souady and Fatima. He tried to be cheerful though the wound paint was intense.

"How are you Cristian? How have you reacted to your baptism of fire?"

"Well, the experience has been strong, but I am trying to turn the page."

"In accordance with our beliefs, having shed our enemy's blood incorporates you definitely to our people. Personally, I have to thank you for having saved my life."

"No a big deal."

"How can you say that? You have pulled me out of the line of fire. Left where I was surely I would not have saved my life. The most important thing has been your spontaneous reaction, just what it was needed. I'm glad that my grandson has your blood."

Ousmar strongly reiterated his gratitude in front of the family so that everyone would be aware of the role of his son-in-law in the combat. Fatima, who knew how to construe well his father words in its personal and political dimensions, could not avoid a gesture of pride. After all she was who had carried this pale and skinny alien into the clan.

The conversation continued on the meaning of the encounter and clash with the Saharans for the village. Ousmar was more worried about that than by his wound. Their thinking was the same that Haroun had anticipated last night.

"Never had they dared so far South. There is no doubt that you have no restrictions and their audacity has grown." Then he paused and added in a bitter tone. "I'm afraid that the question is not whether we are going to a conflict with them but when."

The present heard the premonitory sentence silently; aware of what was at stake in their lives. Ousmar shook his head to ward off pesky thoughts and added.

"I already called a meeting of the tribal Council the day after tomorrow. You'll come." He told Cristian and completed the reflection "I want to hear the thoughts of elders and warriors."

This time Cristian became among the first attendees because he accompanied his father-in-law who was still weak. The members of the Council were arriving, some of them from remote villages because the seriousness of the issue warranted it.

When they had all arrived the oldest of the members made known his desire to be him who opened the meeting, what everyone agreed.

"On behalf of all the present here I want to express our joy for the fact that spirits who govern the destinies of our community have protected our beloved leader of the evil designs of our enemies."

Said that he rose with difficulty, approached the fire around which all participants were gathered together, extracted a handful of dust from a pocket of his robe and threw it at flames which sizzled vividly illuminating the meeting. A strong emotion seized all participants of the silent audience before the symbol loaded with shared meanings.

"It is the shaman of our tribe "Haroun whispered in the ear of Cristian; as it was customary he translated the sayings and the facts of the meeting to the newcomer. The shaman returned to his post in the round but not sat. In a wide gesture pointed to Cristian.

"Also I wish to say that we were not wrong when a short while ago we decided to incorporate to our clan a young foreigner whom we did not know. Today we have reasons to celebrate having done so."

A murmur of approval reflected the consensus of the attendees. Cristian blushed as it was usual in him while a smiling Haroun placed a hand on his shoulder.

Important decisions were made at the plenary. A delegation would go to N'Djamena to talk with a French military acquaintance and explain new developments and urge him to send weapons and troops, although there were not too many expectations on the latest. All those sick, children young or older who had relatives in villages South of Chad would be evacuated towards them in an organized way, since in a possible sudden and forced exodus they would delay the rest exposing them for increased risks. On the perimeter of the village would be built barricades of way to hinder or delay the entry of hostile troops on horseback or in trucks, and finally, ambushes would be organized in certain canyons and gorges leading to the North. Nobody knew if this could save the village but certainly it would cost heavy casualties to potential offenders and give time to evacuate.

A week passed without notable alternatives; a morning Haroun came to pick up Cristian with two horses, sure indication of a short cruise. He made no comments until they were underway.

"We will act as a welcome Committee." He said.

"In what sense?" Asked Cristian somewhat frightened by the ambushes that had been prepared.

"Don't worry." replied Haroun laughing. "We are truly to receive friends."

They remained on high land that allowed a broad vision, particularly towards the North. After three hours they could see dust columns on the misleading horizon.

"Are they real, or it is a mirage?" Asked the young man.

"No, these are real. I guess they are those who we expect. Just in case you prepare your rifle."

When the stains in the desert approached they distinctly saw two large trucks preceded and followed by two jeeps. They had no flags or badges that would tell who they were. However, Haroun said.

"It's they all right. Let's go greet them."

When the two riders approached the gunner who handled a heavy machine gun in the jeep heading the convoy pointed at them, but a white officer who was traveling in the front passenger seat made a gesture.

"*Bienvenue, capitaine Romand.* " Greeted Haroun from a distance.

"Haroun, mon ami "replied the officer.

The two riders dismounted and waited for the vehicles to approach. Captain Romand jumped out of the jeep and hugged Haroun. The warrior introduced Cristian, who however remained at a distance, while the two friends were talking. Then all resumed their march towards the village.

"But are they actually French?" Asked Cristian "Most of them are black skinned."

"They are *légionnaires*."

"Of the Foreign Legion?" Romantic and heroic legends invaded Cristian mind.

"Yes, but do not come from Fort Zinderneuf (1)." Replied jokingly Haroun, realizing the fantasies that passed through the head of his partner. "They are bringing us automatic weapons, ammunition and communications equipment. All former Soviet equipment, to dispel accusations."

"Do the famous AK-47?"

"That's right."

"You can't complain."

"We don't know what those who attack us will bring us but will not waiting our welcome."

(1) refers to the Foreign Legion Fort where takes place the novel Beau Geste, of P.C.Wren

That night Fatima was waiting for her husband in the way that he knew very well. Both had been without physical contact since Cristian returned from the trading excursion with Ousmar, due to the rear shock created by the dramatic events that occurred. Both had since accumulated an unusual dose of unmet sexual needs in their relationship that had to be updated immediately. The woman threw him from a nudge on a large sofa and sat on his knees with legs listed to one side. She stroked his face and head as it was her custom, and kissed him in the mouth. He slipped a hand between the folds of the dress that she wore and long stroked the knees, and finally the thighs. He stopped on the inner side of these, what was the usual detonator of their excitation. She lifted the dress up exposing her exquisitely shaped legs; He leaned and kissed the fleshy thighs up to the crotch. She began to moan. He licked the top of the thighs, while she kissed his nape and neck. The excitement had reached the point that required immediate relief. Cristian rose to his wife in his arms and led her to the bed, while she was opening her shirt. Even before he finished removing his pants and underwear he penetrated her warm and humid inside. Both lovers joined in a frenetic rhythm dotted with groans of Fatima, until both reached a violent and painful climax. Cristian lay on his wife until they managed to restore normal breathing.

"Never leave me for so long." She whispered.

"Not if I can help it, I promise you."

They fell asleep hugged. Cristian awoke first, and was on the bed still streaky with his wife.

A thought assailed from time to time and although he wanted to remove it from his mind he failed to do so. He felt fully realized in his relationship with Fatima. He loved her and could not imagine his life without her. The woman covered all the emotional, intellectual, moral and sexual aspirations a demanding man could have and now were additionally joined by their son. He was fully happy in his marriage, and yet... and yet... was Charfadine.

The infatuation he felt by the young woman was a feeling that was previously unknown to him, despite the fact that in his life before Fatima he had many female relationships. He knew Charfadine would be an open wound that would never close. He unfairly complained of fate which exposed him to these cross feelings. What had happened to that foolish boy who was born as a leave in the wind by insubstantial relationships with women that after a while got tired of maintaining him and disappeared from his life just as fast as they had come? Love had come to his life with a dose of pain.

Cristian rose with caution not to wake his wife. He had an appointment with Haroun, who had anticipated him he had some news after their meeting with the *légionnaires*.

"For the moment and for domestic political reasons France not can deal with us, at least they cannot send troops. The French economic situation does not improve, and voters do not accept expenses abroad, whatever the cause and much less wars that can cause casualties."

"What then?"

"Then we will have to protect ourselves. The problem is that the Muslims receive support in men and weapons from Al Qaeda and financial resources from the Gulf States."

"Do the French bring at least promised weapons?"

"Yes, but they are skimping them; less than promised in quantity and quality. We have now enough automatic weapons, but they brought us a few missiles."

"Although I have a quarter of French blood, I never trusted them." Said Cristian.

"However, in the past they saved us from extermination several times. We would not be here without them. They are our guarantor of last resort. Right now they are tangled in our neighboring Central African Republic, where Christians and Muslims are massacring each other."

"Christians?"

"Yes, they are a majority in the country; most of them are animists converted by missionaries. The French are mediating between fractions and can't get away as demand their politicians."

Both men did a few moments of silence.

"The purpose of our meeting today is to show you the use of the AK-47. Your life and that of your family may depend on it."

Fatima was awakened by the cries of Hubert. She changed clothes and breastfed him, after which the baby fell asleep. Then the woman got a shower because she felt perspired by the sexual exercises the night before. Then she lunched lightly and sat on the sofa in the room.

The thoughts came to mind in droves, and she could not help introspection. Memory receded to his life before meeting Cristian, and when evoking it, she found it empty and devoid of any purpose. In reality, the dedication to the cause of the exiled Chadian was practically everything she had; no personal projects. Several experiences with men had been frustrating and ephemeral. She recalled when she saw Cristian for the first time. The night before she had made a similar self-analysis. A sudden impulse came then from inside that drove her to make the man hers and she had proceeded accordingly in the hotel full of sarcastic passengers. From there the relationship had deepened rapidly in a way that exceeded her best expectations. Cristian and the advent of his son had transformed her life completely and had filled it with sense. There was a loose end of which she had increasingly become aware and which was still puzzling her and looked threatening... but she would face it in due time. It was surely not Fatima who would lose what she had obtained.

Fatima stood up, she knew that this rare episodes of introspection always preludes important turns in her life and that she had to prepare herself to make difficult decisions. These decisions were apt to involve hard choices and trade-offs, and to affect other people's lives. This was her burden.

CHAPTER 10

Ousmar had just opened a small health post at the southern end of the village. It would be attended by a Nigerian doctor who would come twice a week to the village, a standing Chadian paramedic and two Cameroonian nuns. The French had brought some medical equipment and drugs along with weapons, and promised to add more instruments in the future.

"My father has a modernizing mentality." Fatima told her husband. "And he listens to my advice on social matters. His current priorities, along with defense of course, are health and education. If there is more stability in the area we could be of interest to *Medicins sans Frontiers*. In fact our ethnic group was the first of Chad prohibiting genital mutilation of girls."

"You must change the agenda and incorporate issues that are considered important in the world, and replace the primitive beliefs based on wiles and witchcraft." Said impulsively Cristian.

She analyzed her husband's reflection, grimaced and responded with mock anger.

"You should have a little more respect for the primitive beliefs of my people, which I share in part. They have allowed us to survive centuries in which no young Argentine know-it-all wiseacre cared about us, even in times when there were not even Argentineans."

Cristian regretted his pedantic statement, and sought to compensate it. He took her by the waist and she hugged her neck; When the man placed a hand on the buttocks she exhaled a howl.

"Yes, I am already aware of your primitive side, and am grateful that neither Paris nor New York removed it from you.

At that time came a maid with Hubert in her arms, announcing that it was necessary to change his diapers, task which Fatima usually performed personally.

Cristian approached the hut located far away from the center of the village that had been transformed into arsenal and powder keg. Two armed guards were guarding it. They recognized him and let him in. Haroun was inside.

"Some news!" exclaimed jokingly Cristian. "Armed village guards."

"Nothing will be as it was." Said Haroun in somber tone. "At least for a long time."

"Do you remember we said that we would do shooting practice with the AK-47?"

"I have inverted the order a bit. Today I prefer that we learn together the use of the communication equipment the French have brought us. I assign them almost more importance than to weapons."

They had been invited to a party at the house of Ousmar Djalali, organized under some pretext but really had the purpose of giving a welcome to Captain Romand who was a strategic ally of the tribe. Fatima was as usual the host along with her father for her excellent French, while Souady took care of the other guests, thirty members of the top strata of the village and some officers of the Foreign Legion.

Cristian had greeted the military in its rudimentary French, as well as practically every one of the guests who approached him briefly. Then he sat down to observe the party. He looked to his wife, who showed her splendid and slender silhouette in a beautiful dress that was completely unknown to him. Her natural grace and smoothness of movements produced an irrepressible sense of pride in the man. After a while spent in solitude he saw Souady coming in his direction. He rose when she approached and then they sat down together to talk. The lady told him all kinds of details about the life and circumstances of each one of the participants, who she fully knew. Cristian was looking to Romand by comments made by her mother-in-law and noticed that the French glanced an internal door with a gesture of admiration. Following the direction of the eyes of the military Cristian saw that Charfadine had appeared wrapped in a blue dress, no doubt her favorite color, girded at the waist so that it hinted her figure. The image was so shocking that the young man kept his gaze for several seconds while Souady was still talking to him. Making an effort he turned his eyes to his mother-in-law and answered some triviality to what she was saying.

Souady changed the axis of your conversation and also looked at her youngest daughter.

"Is she not beautiful?"

Taken by surprise, the young man slightly blushed and nodded affirmatively.

"When Charfadine was born, Fatima was fifteen years old. My husband and I had already lost the hope of having more children. I must thank Ousmar that he did not take more wives then. The birth of Charfadine was a gift from the gods." Her eyes shone as she recalled her youth. "Just as we had done with Fatima after completing the elementary school in N'Djamena, we send Charfadine to France for his secondary studies in an élite school so she has received a wonderful education that everybody immediately notices. Then she agreed to return here, with her family and people but I think that this is not the environment in which she can flourish at her best." She stopped. "Oh! Here comes Ousmar." Souady then stood up and turned towards her husband leaving Cristian pensive and a bit perplexed. On the one hand he thanked the information on Charfadine and in general about his political family that Souady had given him, since Fatima had never made many references to her family past. On the other hand he wondered what was the reason for which his mother-in-law, with whom he had not had many talks before, had ostensibly sought an opportunity to approach him at the party and make these so intimate confidences. Given the conflictive relationship status in which he was

Cristian, the talk wasn't indifferent for him. He wondered if it was simply a casual conversation or if on the contrary it had an implicit message for him, and in that case, which was that message.

Since Fatima was still occupied in her protocol activities, Cristian went out to the porch and walked a few steps trying to clarify his ideas. As he turned around he saw Charfadine leaving the house and follow in his footsteps in a distracted way. The girl smiled him, and he gave free rein to his feelings.

"Hello Charfadine. You look beautiful today."

The smile of the woman turned flirtatious.

"Only today? Could it be the outfit?"

"No." Cristian coughed and added whispering. "You're a beautiful woman. Few times I've seen..." a lump in the throat prevented him to follow. He looked her perfect countenance, her huge black eyes, straight nose and the lips painted blue. He exhaled a sigh.

"My father would like that you joined the men in a meeting with *le Capitaine Romand*." Replied Charfadine obviously flattered. "The meeting will take place in the tent you already know."

So she was only carrying a message from her father! Although it solved a situation which could become complicated the outcome turned out disappointing for Cristian.

When he arrived the meeting had already begun. He sat as it was his custom beside Haroun. Romand was talking.

"... as I already explained to some of you, France cannot send an additional contingent to Chad. We already have a few thousand men who are moving all the time in this huge country. In the Central African Republic the situation is desperate, the *antibalaka* and the Muslim rebels are gutting each other in the streets and our troops are actively engaged to separate the contenders. In my country the economic situation is deteriorating, the President has lost popular support and is weak and there is no way to justify higher costs overseas."

He paused to take a breath and let his words to take effect. He went on.

"This does not mean however that we are going to leave you to your fate. We have brought a good quantity of modern weapons like the ones your eventual aggressors may have or better, since all come from ancient arsenals of the former Soviet Union. We will reinforce the medical team, and our communication equipments are most advanced. We will maintain permanent contact by radio with you from N'Djamena and informed our superiors in Paris on a regular basis. A new butchery like in Darfur will not be allowed. The world will not accept it! Finally, and although you do not need political advice I can still give you our opinion. It is appropriate that his clan reinforce its links with the rest of the ethnic Sara, since you all are of the same blood and have the same enemies."

This last sentence caused a rumor among the attendees, in general of disapproval. Ousmar anticipated to any adverse demonstration speaking.

"As usual we thank to our friend *le Capitaine Romand* for the valuable material support and advice France is giving us. We value the perspective of keeping in touch with our French allies, especially if the situation deteriorates further."

The French then stood up and expressed.

"This ethnic group is a model in all Chad and the whole Central Africa for your concern for people, your progressive mindset, and the involvement of its members. We will not let this light go off!"

The meeting concluded Ousmar and Haroun accompanied the French military who were riding their jeep and returning to their distant base, whilst the rest of the attendees dispersed strongly arguing about the message received.

A little later Cristian reunited with Haroun, who asked.

"What do you think of Romand´s speech?"

"Hypocrite. You know what I think of the French. They declaim beautiful principles but deny them with their actions."

"Your inexperience makes you to be unfair. A Government must prioritize their actions and manage their financial, physical and psychic resources, always scarce."

"What psychic resources?"

"The State of the opinion public, essential in democracies but always volatile.

"Well, I see that you accept the situation."

"As I already told you, in an extreme case we will have them here. Our lawyers in Paris, Washington and New York will make sure of that, but we have to make our effort here."

Cristian grimaced. He was well aware of Fatima´s action in New York in favor of Chad refugees.

"I still did not like much his recommendation to join the rest of the Sara." Haroun completed his assessment of the meeting.

"That was however the part that sounded more reasonable to me. Why didn't you like it?"

"Because carrying it out would subordinate us to some of the big clans of the ethnic Sara: the Mbaye, the Goulaye, the Kaba and the Ngana."

"That is to say, it does not guarantee the preservation of the role of our clan leaders."

"Among which are you! And I'm glad to hear you talking of our clan."

"It is definitely also my clan. My son already includes also my blood in it."

Haroun festively patted his friend back. His claim had the flavor of a personal success.

At home Cristian found a radiant Fatima. Her participation in all the party had been dazzling, her parents were proud of her and

few doubted that Ousmar leaned in her eldest daughter for the village
government.

The woman asked Cristian to share with her what had happened
in the meeting at the tent. He did it with detailed as possible and she
interrupted him every now and then to ask for clarification on some
points, in particular expressions poured in the conclave.

"Hummm! " She said enigmatically at the end "I think that some of
this will bring consequences."

"What do you mean?"

"To links with the rest of the Sara clans."

"Another bigot. You speak as Haroun."

"What you do not realize is that ethnic ties are not just political.
They have personal implications." Although Cristian was intrigued for
that statement he asked no further explanations.

That afternoon Fatima went with Hubert to her parent's house,
to meet with Ousmar and Souady; she returned late at night, just in
time for dinner with her husband. She did not make any comments
pretexting being very fatigued.

A month later, Cristian was playing with his son, who had already
begun to crawl, when Souady entered the house quite altered. Fatima,
who was in the kitchen, looked out upon hearing the nervous tone of
her mother.

"Take a deep breath." She said, and once achieved its objective
asked. "Now tell us what is happening?"

"Refugees are coming to the village from the North. Muslim
militiamen have ravaged several villages. There are many injured among
those who arrive."

Fatima and Cristian commissioned Souady to stay to care for the
child and went to the northern end of the village to get first hand news.

Men, women and children were located at the edges of the road
and more were permanently arriving on horseback, some old cars and
on foot; the lucky ones brought with them possessions and some goats,

the rest, just the clothes they were wearing. Cristian saw Haroun from afar; he was surrounded by a group of his men trying to help those who arrived. The warrior called him with a gesture and the young man was to trot where his friend was. Fatima joined a group of women distributing water among the refugees, being that the first necessity after dehydrate hours or days along the Sahel. The first aid room staff was already taking care of those who arrived injured, but the capacity of the venue was already filled.

While Fatima was distributing water and some food heard the stories of murder, rape, fire and horror of the displaced. She saw her father deeply shocked organizing the help with the scarce resources of the village. A deep emotion, between despair and pride nested in the breast of the woman. She approached Ousmar who as he saw her only managed to say.

"They will pay for it. They will not get away with it."

"You must contact Romand immediately and let he know what is happening."

In moments of a great commotion, Ousmar thanked to have his eldest daughter beside him., able to keep a cool head in the most distressing moments, Fatima was exactly the psychic reserve that the leader needed in that moment. He hugged her strongly and a few tears appeared in the eyes of the old warrior.

"You cannot break down now." She said. "Now all depend on your orders and example."

The next day two helicopters descended on the desert plain to the North of the village. Their insignia were covered and only its camouflaged fuselage could be seen. Soldiers that descended from it had no identification either. Ousmar led an African Lieutenant to the refugee camp which had been erected in pitiful conditions by some groves and near a water spring.

"How many people are there? Have you counted them?" Asked the officer, visibly shocked.

"One thousand three hundred twenty-." "Responded Haroun before an inquisitive look of Ousmar.

"Wounded?

"One hundred fifty, of which twenty-six have serious injuries."

"Relatively few."

"We do not know how many have been left in the desert."

"Well, now we've brought 10 paramedics and plenty of medical equipment, some additional heavy weapons, and two tons of rice. In three days we will return."

"What will say it to your superiors?"

"I will show them an accurate picture of what is happening. We are indeed filming the camp and we need all the hard data that you have on the situation."

"Among the refugees have arrived some two hundred fit men." Added Haroun." We are going to incorporate them into our militia. We need weaponry for them."

"I will have that into account."

Fatima watched the scene from a distance. She knew that crucial days were approaching and that she needed to make plans for her people and her family.

CHAPTER 11

Cristian observed the row of new recruits while waiting for the moment of their entry into action. As that the majority of them spoke only Arabic or Chadian dialects, the young man would be in charge of the magazine of uniforms, weapons control and shooting practices where he could make understood only with signs.

The majority of selected refugees were very young, following an old and sad African tradition of children-soldiers. Few had any military training since they had been shepherds of goats, but they were superb horsemen and knew better than Cristian how to guide a camel. A detail that impressed him was their absent gaze, their lost expressions, possibly still under the weight of experienced hardships, something like the post-traumatic shock of certain war wounded. It didn't cost him much to guess the burden of hatred that nested under the veil of stupor. If there would be fighting, it would be to kill or be killed.

When Haroun freed him from his task, he returned home, finding that Fatima had gone, leaving the child in charge of Haiwanda, one of the maids. The girl informed him that the Lady had left two hours earlier, and that she had gone to her parents. It was unusual that his wife left the child only with maids for extended periods of time so he guessed something thick would be preparing at Djalali home.

Fatima returned still an hour later, and when her husband questioned her about the purpose of the meeting replied evasively pretexting a headache, a traditional excuse women use to avoid themes or actions. Cristian decided not to insist knowing that ultimately he would learn what happened one way or another.

That night, while they were eating supper, Fatima decided to spontaneously share some of what had been spoken. However Cristian realized that there was something that bothered her.

"Has been an emissary of a tribal chieftain of the clan Mbaye with certain proposals and conditions for his support in the event of an attack." She said, and then remained silent.

"Well?"asked Cristian.

"Well, nothing. My father will evaluate the conditions."

"And have you given some opinion?"

"No, no, nothing in particular."

Given that she would him nothing more, he ceased in asking. As he realized that his wife was entering her feline phase he decided to take advantage of it; at least it would shake from the mind of both the bad shots of the day.

The next day as Cristian met Haroun he questioned him somewhat abruptly about what happened in the meeting with the clan Mbaye.

"As I have not been present I have no firm version, only a few transcended comments. The Sougui chief delegate raised some conditions to support us with his clansmen in case of aggression."

He looked at him rummaging through his head how to follow.

"The conditions seem to include the appointment of one of his delegates overseeing our tribal council meetings, the subordination of all our troops to a captain sent by him and delivery of twenty virgins to marry his son and his lieutenants including ..."

"¿Including whom?" Cristian asked anxiously.

It was obvious that Haroun would rather circumvent the answer.

"Well ... they are just versions."

"¿Including whom?" Insisted the young man.

"Well" Haroun sighed. "Including Charfadine. Her beauty could not go unnoticed."

Cristian was invaded by a wave of emotions that showed in his face, which turned livid. Haroun immediately became aware of it.

-¿You know what response has given Ousmar?"

"I think only evasive."

Cristian tried to pull himself together and put his ideas in order. He finally asked.

"What do you think that it will happen with these demands?"

"On the one hand the Mbaye are powerful and have a large and well-armed, militia even though I have my doubts about the readiness of their reaction in the event of an attack, given their distance to our village. I'm not sure of how fiercely they would combat for us. On the other hand, Chief Sougui is proud and I do not know how he would take a negative by Ousmar. It is a difficult position given the implications."

"What implications do you mean?

"The loss of power of our Council and Ousmar, the lack of control over our own warriors... and the situation of Charfadine and other young women."

Haroun realized the state of bewilderment that the news had brought on Cristian, and did everything possible to calm him down. He decided not to continue with the concealment, since he had enough confidence and ascendancy over Cristian.

"Don't worry about Charfadine. The case is in the hands of Ousmar, who is both the father and a true negotiator. He will know how to fix this snare of destiny. Be confident in our leader."

They were arriving at the site where recruits were waiting for them to continue with the training.

"Take a charge from the control of the guns." Haroun ordered.

Cristian returned home crestfallen. He could not accept the idea that Charfadine was delivered to another man, when he knew perfectly the young girl's feelings for him. At the same time, his own feelings were exposed, freed from the moral conscious repression by the shock of the news. He could not accept that a question of love would be subject to state reasons.

Fatima saw him arriving and not even tried to talk to him; she knew too well what was happening to her husband.

One of the watchmen was the first is to see them. In the distance, almost on the desert horizon several clouds of dust were approaching.

Cristian looked at Haroun and soothed at seeing his friend's attitude.

"There are too few to be a danger." Said the war chief as guessing the thoughts of the young man.

Indeed, half an hour later five members of the militia arrived under the command of a young lieutenant named Abakar. They were carrying another man on top of a sixth horse, injured and tied down, obviously a prisoner.

"We had a strong clash with a patrol of some fifteen Goran tribesmen, we could finally reject them, we lost five men and they four and we took this wounded dog."

"Well, bring him to Ousmar. He will know what to do, we need all the information you can get. I am already sending reinforcements in case the Goran come back.

Abakar and four of his men continued their travel and Haroun ordered ten of his men accompany the fifth rider to the border in the desert.

"How are you going to interrogate the wounded man?" Asked Cristian, sensing the response.

"You do not want to know." Was the laconic reply.

Upon returning home, Cristian found Fatima breast-feeding her child. Just as he talked only a few words with her, he realized that there was a change in her attitude, less contractured and tense. The young man was very sensitive to his wife's moods and had noticed that lately she had been under strong tension, which exacerbated his own discomfort. He decided not to ask about something as subjective as this impression and left time to clarify it.

When she finished feeding Hubert, Fatima approached her husband and kissed him on the cheek. She knew how much he was aware of her signs of affection.

"Ah!" She told him as passing. "My father has called a family meeting for tomorrow. All will attend."

"Am I invited?"

"Of course; you already know your position in the family."

CRISTIAN GLIMPSED A carrion birds flitting about three hundred meters from the site where he was. With some frequency there were carcasses of camels, horses or goats abandoned in the desert, so that already knew what kind of spectacle he was going to find. Anyway he felt that he had to go to investigate so he delegated command to Abakar and led his horse towards the place.

Arriving near felt that stomach churned him realizing that the remains were human. Overcoming his disgust he approached and saw with horror that it was a body completely disfigured and covered in blood, whose hands had been cut off and his chest open in channel. Vomiting finally arrived and he was bent in two for a few moments. He immediately recognized by the clothes who the man had been. It was the prisoner who had been taken the previous day by Abakar and his men, and who had been carried to the village. The fact did not surprise him because he had already anticipated the reactions, particularly of refugees who had arrived a fortnight ago. The struggles in the desert had a load of ferocity for which Cristian was not mentally prepared.

He returned to the place where his detachment was and ordered Abakar that to bury the remains. The Lieutenant argued that it had been left there to be seen, to serve as I warning to potential attackers and to deter them, but Cristian did not compromise and reiterated his strict order to bury the body.

What most bothered the young man was the consciousness that the barbaric execution could not have happened without participation of Ousmar. He also knew that any complaint that he could make to Ousmar, Haroun or even Fatima was doomed to failure. The only option was to shut up, and know that silence turned him into an accomplice.

The next morning Cristian and Fatima went to the Djalali house. The woman had left Hubert with the maid and her husband had requested Haroun to replace him in his task.

Ousmar, Souady and a couple of younger brothers of the Chief were already assembled. Charfadine was not present.

Without any preambles Ousmar began to speak.

"The reason for this meeting is to explain the grounds of the answer that I must give to the demands of the Chief of the clan Mbaye. I have already consulted with all the elders and I have made my decision. Tomorrow we will make it official in the tribal Council."

Then he began to explain the decisions taken and their rationale.

"We cannot accept that they appoint a delegate to participate in our tribal councils because he would become the power behind the throne, to give him a name, and our decisions rather than favoring our people would be serving other interests and a different agenda." Ousmar did a brief respite. "The same criteria apply to the claim of our militia being subordinated to an external chief."

Ousmar was detailing one by one the decisions taken, which coincided in general with what Haroun had anticipated to Cristian. The man was tense waiting for the rest of the topics, notably the fate of Charfadine. He looked briefly at Fatima whose moods he had learned to read accurately and saw her serene, that feeling that somehow was transmitted to his spirit.

"Last but most important." Continued Ousmar. "We have the theme of the women who the Mbaye asked us to give them. We will ask the potential candidates if any of them wants to join the Mbaye. Otherwise the answer will be negative."

Here, Cristian had a break; things were moving in the desired direction.

"A special case is that of my daughter Charfadine." Ousmar's voice almost broke here. "This issue was of the utmost importance for Chief Mbaye, since a dynastic union would mean their future domain. It is therefore a very important goal for the Mbaye, and a negative response would be expensive for us in terms of external support."

Ousmar made a stop; Cristian felt that his head was spinning around. Fatima stared at him to analyze his reactions.

"But I will not deliver my daughter against her will." Ousmar continued talking, Cristian produced a notorious exhalation. The head continued. "There is a unique way to deal with this it without seriously offending the Mbaye."

Ousmar silences had the purpose to underline the reasons and consequences of their decisions, but had the young man in suspense.

"To achieve our goals without consequences Charfadine must be married and this marriage has to be consummated. This will put an end to the interest of the Mbaye Chief."

Cristian felt that his head exploited. Charfadine married? How and with whom? Fatima came up and stroked the head of her husband increasing his confusion.

Ousmar had completed his presentation and rose to leave. Cristian had an impulse to stop him to ask for clarifications, but restrained it. The chief finally left the family meeting.

As in a well planned scenery Charfadine entered the room, and the young man's heart accelerated. Just at that time realized that her sister-in-law had been absent while her future was being debated, but Cristian had no time to continue with his musings.

"Please, listen to me!"

The family assembly continued, and Souady was now in charge....

CHAPTER 12

The meeting had been reduced to Souady, Fatima, Charfadine, and Cristian; somehow, those directly interested in the further course of events.

"The Chief has spoken." expressed Souady. "and has ruled what should be the fate of Charfadine in accordance with the interests of our clan. My daughter should be married to avoid snubbing Mbaye clan and therefore the whole Sara ethnicity. It is not Ousmar Djalali's function of determine who has to marry Charfadine. As his mother and it is no secret that she's my favorite daughter, I will take the situation in my hands from here on.

The girl's cheeks blushed. She had certainly never thought that her future would be subject to so many pressures of the political and ethnic environment.

"As her mother, it is my duty to ensure that no husband that she does not love is imposed to Charfadine is. That is, she must choose her husband freely, of course, by common accord. Tell us daughter, who is the man you love?"

The girl remained silent. The mother repeated the question with identical result.

"It is clear that my sister has imposed silence by her desire not to impact other lives." Fatima said unexpectedly. "But we all know what her heart dictates. We know that Charfadine loves my husband Cristian, and that he loves her."

The man jumped in his place, he couldn't believe what he had just heard, particularly from his wife's mouth. Of all people, he would have never thought that Fatima said those words knowing how she loved him.

Souady was now speaking again.

"Charfadine, do you love Cristian Colombo and accept to be his wife?"

""Yes."

"Charfadine, do you love Cristian Colombo and accept to be his wife?"

"Yes."

"Charfadine, do you love Cristian Colombo and accept to be his wife?

"Yes!

"Well." Said Souady "That part of the ritual has been completed. The woman has accepted three times to marry the proposed man."

Then she turned to Cristian, but this interrupted her with a gesture.

"Souady, we all know that I'm married to your eldest daughter and I am your grandson's father, how could I then marry Charfadine?"

"Fatima "Souady asked his eldest daughter "Would you accept that your husband marry your sister?"

"I accept it." said the woman. "But I think it's fair to tell him about our customs regarding marriage."

Then Souady went on to explain his son-in-law that polygamy was permitted in Chad and that a man can marry more than once in the bosom of the Sara ethnic group, and that if he married his sister-in-law not only was not frowned upon but it facilitated things. The condition was not to neglect his first wife and her offspring. In fact, one in three Chadian women lives in families with situations of polygamy.

"Said this, Cristian Colombo, I ask you: do you love my daughter Charfadine and want to take her in marriage?"

"Yes." the man answered without hesitation.

"Well." Continued Souady. "Now I just have to inform Ousmar Djalali about this decision to since it is he who must give our daughter in marriage."

The family meeting concluded there. Cristian was puzzled by its development, since he concluded that it's real purpose had been to arrange the marriage between Charfadine and him, obtaining their mutual explicit consent to meet with ethnic traditions. It was equally obvious that everything was prepared in advance and the only ones who weren't aware were just Charfadine and he. When Cristian could finally put in order his ideas he realized that this decision filled his aspirations since he could share his destiny with the two women he loved, so he could not ask life any more. However, it spurred the doubt of how driven by love but also for reasons of State which he, Cristian, did not understand nor justify. Yet the fact that a woman as possessive as Fatima consented to share her husband, even with her sister exceeded his understanding capacity. He made a long turn to reach back home in order to have more time to think about how to address his wife.

Fatima was waiting for him with the child in her arms, with a somewhat sad gesture in her countenance. Cristian made no comments, leaving his wife to take the initiative, as it usually happened.

"Well." She finally said. "Is there anything you want to know?"

"Of course. I appreciate your detached gesture, but I do not understand how and why you have agreed to share me."

"I have not agreed it was really my initiative."

The response baffled even more the young man who after a few moments, said.

"So it is your will to share me."

"Not really. It was a realistic decision. My father conceived the idea of marrying Charfadine to save her from a horrible future."

"And prevent the Mbaye to be masters of your clan."

"Also that. Then my mother put on the table what we all already knew, that Charfadine and you love each other. This is a fact of life; it is not the creation of my parents or my own."

"And you simply accepted the facts of life?"

"It is not that the idea pleased me, but I was convinced that it was the best thing for everyone. Of course I know that it is the best for my sister and for you."

"And what takes a woman to share her husband?"

"I know well that there are differences between the male and the female, the male is polygamous by nature, and you can love two women at the same time more easily than a woman can love two men. But I will tell you clearly what brought me to make this specific decision. A woman fear is the possibility of losing her man. I am sure that this will not happen, that you will continue loving me. I have no doubt in this regard."

"So that I can be taken for granted?"

Fatima, who so far had spoken without tension but serious now smiled, pushed her husband to the armchair and sat on his legs, as she used to do.

"So it is, and there is nothing you can do about it. I'm stuck inside of you."

Cristian did not respond he could recognize a truth when he heard it."

Souady made preparations to carry out the wedding with utmost urgency. Indeed, when Ousmar communicated the Mbaye boss that his daughter was already married, it had to be true.

"This situation unfortunately leaves no time to now make a wedding as your sister's." She told Charfadine. "But I am confident that once everything settles down we can carry out a ceremony as you deserve."

She stood next to her daughter who was sitting, took her head and pressed it against her side. Charfadine was Souady's favorite daughter who was also her lawyer advocate in all circumstances.

"The important thing is that you marry a man who will make you happy, I know he will."

HAROUN POINTED TO AN object in the dunes ahead of them and ordered one of his men to come closer.

"It has a metallic sheen." Said Cristian who was riding beside him.

"It must be remnants of some vehicle. But keep telling me about the family reunion."

The young man finished telling him what had happened in the conclave, but refrained from telling him the subsequent intimate talk with his wife. Haroun meditated and finally his friend.

"Well, what do you think of all this?"

"Ousmar´s decision to marry his daughter seems right and daring at the same time. In this way he does not cut relations with another clan in moments of peril. The role of Souady of favoring the choice of Charfadine was predictable coming from a protective mother." New silence.

"And what about Fatima´s role?"

"Hmm! It is also shareable and predictable, coming from a smart woman d with strong leader skills as your wife."

Predictable! Why do you say it?

"Don´t you realize the implications?" Answered Haroun smiling.

"Yes. What you said about not offending the Mbaye and all that stuff."

"Not only that. They could also have married Charfadine, a particularly beautiful woman, with a member of our village."

"And what is your conclusion?"

"Marrying her with you Fatima has closed the path to a possible powerful competitor who might whisper at her father´s ear."

A certain disappointment gripped Cristian; Haroun had opened his eyes to a point that he had overlooked.

"So by controlling me she also controls her sister."

Haroun realized his friend´s new mood and added.

"But don't feel disappointed. Think that at the same time she has secured your happiness and that of her sister. It is a very smart move, and where the only cost is ultimately paid for by Fatima herself.

Cristian admired his companion's lucidity who not only was introducing him in the rules of combat in the desert but also in political and courtiers games that were so alien to him.

"It is true; she pays a cost to maintain her position." But then he recalled her words about her certainty to retain him; the cost was relative and was actually only to yield some exclusive rights on his person.

Then the man who had been sent to recognize the origin of brightness returned with an old auxiliary fuel tank in the hand.

"It's all rusty said Haroun." It must have been years in the desert. It has no importance."

Cristian sighed relieved; lately the finds in the desert had been particularly unpleasant.

Three days later between Charfadine and Cristian was celebrated. The ceremony was similar to the previous marriage with Fatima but much shorter, and was completed in one day. The joy of the wedding was evident, despite its reserved nature. She wore a long white dress in a very rich fabric and a turban of the same color and material.

Finished the entertainment to the attendees the bride and groom along with Souady and Fatima went to the house belonging to the latter and Cristian that had been conditioned to be inhabited by three people.

There they sat down to rest from the fatigue of the day and Fatima showed her sister site which had been very well arranged, given the limited available time.

"Once you are inside you will accommodate it yourself." She expressed.

Finally Souady stood up to return to home, and while Fatima was preparing the child to join her mother and leave the new couple alone, Souady muttered to Cristian with his usual effrontery.

"Do not forget that the marriage must be consummated soon."

Despite the blush that covered his face, this replied in the same mood.

"Don't worry. I won't forget that. I hope you have no complaints from me in that aspect so far, and you will not have them in the future."

"I have none, and that's that I've advocated for you at all times."

When they were finally left alone, Charfadine and Cristian looked at, each other, perhaps for the first time without concealment. A newlywed couple who had until their marriage no moment of intimacy what was very odd thing for him, while for the girl was only the consequence of the wedding customs of her tribe and thus nothing strange.

Cristian approached her slowly, leaving the woman time to adapt to his presence and proximity; he wished to avoid being invasive. She then dedicated him a sweet smile, which made the young go forward more determined. He placed his face close to his wife's and posed his lips upon. They joined in a very long and passionate kiss while the girl overcame her last inhibitions.

"You know." She said. "At my age women of my village have been long married."

"Why have you not done so before?"

"I was waiting for you."

Cristian kissed her neck and began to advance on her shoulders while one of his hands lifted up the skirt of the wedding dress and began to caress her unbeaten flesh. Arriving at her thighs, she issued a soft groan which excited both even more. Cristian awkwardly disrobed his wife untangling the complicated wedding attire, and began to caress and kiss her body, from the top down and then in the opposite direction. Contact of the hands and lips of the man with all of her skin made Charfadine writhe of joy. In a first and prolonged union each came to climax at his own time. Finally they lay in bed still in ecstasy. Charfadine sighed; all her fantasies for her wedding night had been fulfilled.

"Now your mother needs no longer remind me about consummations." he said slyly.

"Just hope that you keep consummating:"

"It not only depends on me."

"I cannot take the initiative, what would you think of me?"

"On the contrary, I would be very pleased if you did. You can get advice with your sister."

"I would die of shame!"

"In fact nobody can give you better tips about me. I will ask to give you advice."

"However, I would rather discover you by myself."

"Just as I have discovered you."

"But you've done it all at once."

Cristian was thrilled with the open relationship which was established with his new wife, as he had feared to have married a prudish and distant lady. Charfadine was surprised for how quickly she had gotten used to intimacy."

CHAPTER 13

"I hope not be riding next to a weakened man as result of his second wedding night." Smilingly said Haroun as he watched his friend yawning.

"I assume that you have experience in this second wedding business."

"In second and third."

One of Haroun subordinates approached galloping saying that he had sighted a contingent of men on camel approaching by Northwest.

"Well, let´s get closer with caution."

The little platoon paused when they saw approaching the camel caravan.

"Their leader is Zakaria, an old fox friend of mine." Stated Haroun.

"What is this friend of yours, robber, bandit and smuggler?" Asked Cristian.

"I do not know with certainty, but I imagine that he has cut a few gorges in his youth."

Haroun approached the caravan leaving his men behind in order not to frighten the caravan members and trigger any undesirable and unnecessary reaction. He was talking to Zakaria for a while and then returned with his men, as his face showed a worried gesture.

"So, what has Zakaria seen that afflicts you?" Sued Cristian.

"It is not what he has seen, but what he has not seen what worries me."

"How is that?"

"They have already been traveling two days without seeing a single soul through the desert."

"And isn´t that why they call it desert?"

"As everybody travels more or less along the same paths, you always find someone on your road. Now the desert is empty."

"And what does that indicate?"

"A possible explanation is that they are running rumors of dangers and conflicts, and people keep away from the roads."

Fatima, Souady and Charfadine had gathered in the daughter's house, and as usual it was the mother who was guiding the course of the conversation, with her usual effrontery.

"So the skinny proved to be quite vigorous." She asked Charfadine in a tone of statement rather than a question.

The girl blushed is and looked down.

"Well." The mother went on. "this is in agreement with your sister´s experience, is it not true Zouby?"

"You know that I wouldn´t have brought him here otherwise." Responded the daughter with equal ironic harshness.

"Fatima, you have squeezed the Italian to obtain pleasure. I want to tell your sister your experiences."

"Oh! That´s enough." Exclaimed Charfadine covering her face in shame.

Souady moved away towards the kitchen uttering laughter. In the background she was delighted with that her favorite child was opening the shell in such a manner.

"Come." Fatima told his sister taking her by the waist "I will tell you some of my tricks. Cristian loves when you surprise him with your requirements. I remember once..."

Fatima, who had always despised her teammates in the New York gym when they described their sexual experiences with their husbands lovers and boyfriends, now found herself doing the same with her own sister.

When they returned that afternoon to the village, Haroun and Cristian were summoned to a tent donated by the French, where they had installed a kind of command, including the equipment of communications from the same source. There were waiting them Ousmar and his four lieutenants, elderly men of warrior extraction who were of his utmost confidence.

"I received a call from Captain Romand." Said the chief bluntly. "Their satellites showed displacements through the desert heading south, then confirmed by a plane especially sent that managed to photograph them. It is a caravan of around thirty trucks, several smaller vehicles and about three hundred to four hundred camels with men and supplies. In sum, a small army in March.

"Between one thousand and one thousand and five hundred men." Haroun had quickly made the math. "Where are they?"

Ousmar went to a large table where a large map of the center of Africa was deployed. With a finger marked a position.

"For a large and slow caravan, a couple of days away from our village." Reflected Haroun "provided they don't do other stops along the way or deviate."

Cristian realized that when a military crisis approached, his friend played a decisive role and that the other hierarchs respected his opinion.

"We have to assume the worst possible scenario and assume that they come for us..." Haroun continued."... and put our troops and our clan on maximum alert."

The conclave had a brief discussion and finally all members accepted the Haroun´s position and began to plan its implementation. Each of those present should take the necessary preventions in their ample circle of relationships to implement what had been agreed.

That afternoon Ousmar showed up in Fatima´s house and got together with his two daughters and his son-in-law.

"Cristian, have you commented with your family what agreed this morning in the tent?" He demanded, not as a relative but as a military commander.

"No, Sir, I did not want to alarm prematurely to Fatima and Charfadine, until you give the order to announce it in the entire village."

Ousmar made a brief summary of the communication of the French and the decisions taken. As he ended Ousmar addressed directly Cristian.

"Cristian, you are responsible for the fate of my daughters and grandson, and with them of the future of our clan. You have to devise in advance a plan for the evacuation of your family and put it into practice when the time comes, what will unfortunately be rather sooner than later."

Charfadine began to cry silently, while Fatima reacted strongly.

"I'll never agree to leave my parents and my people at moments of danger."

Ousmar proudly smiled and kissed her daughter on the forehead.

"No, I'm not asking it as a parent, Fatima, I'm ordering it as your boss."

There was a long discussion in dialect between the father and his daughters that escaped to the understanding of Cristian. When it waned, Fatima translated it.

"We have agreed to evacuate. We've added to my mother among those who will be evacuated. She will be opposed to leave her husband, but my father will force her as he did with us."

"Do you remember Yusuff?" Asked Ousmar to Cristian referring to his personal bodyguard, who had accompanied Ousmar and him them on the trade mission.

The young man nodded with a shudder, recalling the fierce character which had finished off the two fallen aggressors.

"I will put him at your service, accountable to me with his head for your safety. In short, you Cristian will organize the evacuation of my family and look for a safe destination, and Yusuff will look after your backs."

The appointed companion produced mixed reactions; Fatima was glad because she knew the courage and the loyalty of the man towards his father, Charfadine tried to hide her fear and rejection that the character, somewhat sinister caused her, while Cristian, although also Yusuff caused him concern, based on his previous experience celebrated having him taking care of their backs.

Ousmar made available to Cristian a previously unknown and ancient Land Rover with three rows of seats that could therefore accommodate six adult travelers and some luggage. The vehicle had two additional fuel tanks attached to its rear door, and a luggage rack in its broad ceiling, allowing the passengers to load some personal effects if necessary. The four wheels were relatively new while the extra tire was quite worn. In short it deserved Cristian's approval who took a drive test around the village.

The two women began to prepare the luggage they would need in case of a sudden evacuation of which the young man rejected more than half for exceeding the load capacity of the automotive. Souady brought her bags to her daughter's home, to have them ready if necessary. An atmosphere of emergency dyed all the preparations.

Ousmar endowed them with one of the precious equipment of communications with its batteries, and maps of the region. Haroun was present and reviewed with Cristian the exit plan and observed the dedicated elements, expressing his approval.

"I see that you have good organization skills." Said the warrior in a rare compliment to Cristian. "Much will depend on this condition and your ability to improvise."

"Should the need for escape arise." Answered the young man.

"Cristian." Said the warrior in a bitter tone. "The problem is not if it arises but when."

Then he indicated on the map the route of flight, heading Southeast towards Cameroon.

"Remember Hassan?" Asked.

"The old desert rascal friend of yours?

"That man, as he has scented the danger and has migrated south and has established there, on your escape route." Haroun pointed a spot in the map. "He will be waiting with supplies and fuel. He will give you your contacts from there on."

Cristian, initially overwhelmed by the responsibility to take care of all his loved ones in particularly difficult circumstances, was soothing as he saw the progress of the preparations.

That night Cristian entered the bedroom he shared with Fatima, who was already in bed and was preparing to go to bed.

"Wait." Said his wife in imperative tone. "Charfadine is alone in her room and is she very scared. Stay with her."

Without saying a word the young man did as directed. Opening the door he saw that the girl was sitting in bed with her eyes wiped in tears. Always in silence, Cristian removed her footwear, kissed her feet, took her negligee out leaving her beautiful naked body; then he lay down beside her, and began to stroke her gently until the young woman got asleep. Her gesture had changed and a smile emerged on their lips, who know out of what dreams.

Without making any noise, Cristian returned to the bedroom with Fatima, who was waiting for him awake and naked. When he lay also naked on the bed, she swirled around her husband.

"Love me desperately." She said "We do not know what is to come, or when or where we will be able to do it again."

After Fatima got also asleep exhausted of pleasure, Cristian could not help thinking of her attitude of sending him to calm her little sister before meeting her own needs. As it happened once and again a sense of pride and admiration for his wife travelled through his body, and he also slept.

The next morning heavy knocks on the house door woke up the women and Cristian. This stood up bare-chested to open. Yusuff appeared at the door and with unflappable tone said.

"They are coming Be prepared immediately." In a gesture practiced mentally before, Cristian collected the suitcases and placed them on the roof of the truck, tied them up and covered with canvas to keep out the dust from roads. Fatima finished breast-feeding the child while Charfadine brought their staff.

Cristian mounted in the vehicle and drove to his in-laws to pick up Souady. She was already in the House door saying goodbye to her husband with her face flooded in tears. Cristian also loaded her suitcases on the roof, while the Lady put in the cabin food that she had prepared for the trip.

Uncertain of how to proceed the boy approached his father-in-law. This unexpectedly took him in his arms and shook him. "I trust my family to you. Take care of them. My blessings upon you." Strong emotions cut his breath but he continued. "Go now! I have to take care of the defense of my people."

Cristian returned home with Souady on board, there were waiting Charfadine and Fatima with the small Hubert in arms. The man observed his young wife looking desperately through the rear window of the vehicle, seeing as all that knew and loved was left behind. Fatima had her sight fixed forward, as Souady wept in silence. Passing through an intersection he saw Haroun who greeted them with his hand. Cristian made a gesture to stop but his friend urged him to continue driving. At the exit of the village Yusuff waited with his rifle and a backpack for all baggage. Cristian stopped the car, and the man threw the backpack over the ceiling and came up through the back door, between the numerous junk.

In a bend as he was driving with all the speed that the old vehicle was capable of the young looked out of the corner of the eye to the town where he had lived the last year, where he had married and where his son was born, and that now lay already inexorably behind. With a sigh he straightened the car toward their uncertain fate.

CHAPTER 14

Cristian led by badly drawn paths that ran through the last stretches of semi-deserted area of the Sahel, which was imperceptibly turning into the African savannahs. The population density was increasing gradually as the dryness of the landscape gave rise to a higher fertility. Herds of goats and some heads of cattle were grazing around isolated huts, clustering later in small villages.

They entered an area of rolling hills covered with grasses, which at times gained in height. Fatima, Charfadine, Souady and Hubert slept, relaxed once the stress caused by the abrupt departure was over. Only Yusuff remained alert exchanging some words with Cristian, to ensure that the driver was not defeated by the drowsiness.

Where had emerged the mounted figures from they never found out. Yusuff shouted abruptly waking up the women and startling the driver.

"There, on the left! Five gunmen." Immediately he cocked the rifle and poked it through the vehicle window, which he had just opened.

Cristian looked with the corner of his eye, and saw indeed five men mounted on horses and wielding rifles; clearly distinguished that they were approaching and one of them pointed them with his weapon.

The first shot passed above the truck but the following came one after the other. The glass of a window was shattered, and pieces of glass rained down on the women who were sitting in the second row of seats. Charfadine yelled desperate while her mother covered her terrified face. Fatima, who squeezed his son against her breast, found the forces to caress her sister head as she spoke gently to comfort her. Cristian accelerated while he drove along a non-linear path to offer an elusive target. Yusuff tried to fire but the crazy rattle of the Land

Rover and the horsemen galloping wouldn't let he take aim. The vehicle approached at full speed that the old engine could give a narrow gorge between two high cliffs while the riders galloped after them. Suddenly, a man armed with a rifle pointing them emerged at one side of the gorge. Again, Cristian reacted under pressure instantly. With a steering wheel coup he pulled the van out of its course and headed it straight towards the rock wall where the attacker was waiting for them. When he saw the danger coming over him he tried to escape, but the rock did not provide the chance of pulling back. The impact of the car at full speed threw the body crushed by air falling then on the vehicle roof with a terrifying noise. At the last moment with other steering coup in the opposite direction Cristian drove the vehicle back on the road without being able to completely dodge the granite wall, which damaged the rear right side. The damaged car moved in an erratic way scaring women travelling in it. Cristian looked back by the rear view mirror and found that riders were still in pursuit of them, ever closer. At a bend in the road where Cristian had to slow down, Yusuff opened the rear door of the automotive and threw himself on the hard stones from the ground. Looking back through the mirror Cristian saw the brave tribesman beckoning him to continue driving, and then sheltering behind a rock. After a moment of hesitation he decided to continue in order not to compromise the safety of his family and then return to try to help their comrade in his desperate quest. Shots were heard, accounting for the furious battle that unfolded behind them in spite of the distance the truck was travelling. All were paying attention to the fighting sounds until they ceased completely. Charfadine issued a moan; Souady shook her head while Fatima looked down. Cristian whispered a prayer for their brave defender but kept stepping on the accelerator increasing the distance which separated them from their persecutors.

After five hours of silent and sorry travel they approached the point where Hassan was supposed to be waiting for them according to the instructions given by Haroun.

There, they got out of the van to get lunch, under the shadow of an extendable awning which the Land Rover had attached to its roof. The heat was stifling, given the hour and the fact that they were heading towards the Ecuador course. The lunch was silent and full of sorrow. To the uncertainty about the fate of the village and the loved ones added the certainty of what happened with his courageous advocate Yusuff, who sacrificed his life to give them chances to escape. Fatima changed and breastfed her son and all prepared to wait for Hassan, begging that the old man did not fail to appear.

It was mid-afternoon when the inhabitant of the desert- turned into sedentary villager of savannahs- showed up. He asked about Yusuff, whom he certainly knew by their raids through the endless Sahara dunes, and was saddened to learn of his fate.

They accompanied him to his house, indeed little more than the tent in which he lived in the Sahara; there the man handed them over the food, water and fuel at the price agreed with Haroun. Finally, he instructed Fatima and Cristian about the course to follow through the southeast of Chad and Cameroon until they reached the position of their following contact, already in the territory of the latter country.

Cristian tried in vain call by radio the command center that had been established in the village, which increased the shocked climate of the travelers. Only Fatima and Cristian tried to cope with the uncertainty with a somewhat artificial zest.

"We have not run so many dangers to die on the road." Fatima said with a conviction that she actually didn't feel, while she supported her left on the shoulder of her sister, while on the right she held Hubert. Cristian watched them from a distance while he tried to straighten out the battered side of the Land Rover with the help of Hassan. Again he felt admiration for the woman who in the midst of uncertainty had resources to encourage her peers. No doubt, the blood of his father flowed in Fatima's veins and her attitudes showed her leadership conditions in each desperate condition.

Approximately at four o'clock in the afternoon they resumed the journey, having eluded the warmer hours of the torrid day seeking to harness the remaining hours of daylight.

Journey through Cameroon lasted fourteen hours divided into three stages. They stopped wherever they could get minimum guarantees of hygiene and comfort, particularly taking into account that they had to take care of the child.

They finally arrived at the port of Douala, where they stayed in a hotel that gave them some comfort. There Souady and Fatima made contact with Chadians of his same ethnicity residing in Cameroon from years, in order to obtain news of the events in Chad and arrange a ship travel heading to Europe for the whole family.

The two women became worried about the news had been received of compatriots. Chad was plunged into war and confusion. Arab and Islamized groups had made a deep incursion into the territories of the Sahel and the plain to the South of it, destroying villages, killing and looting. The resistance of the inhabitants had been tenacious, desperate and surprisingly organized, so that the fierce fighting had yielded hundreds and perhaps thousands of dead including many raiders, and displaced persons were counted by tens or hundreds of thousands. There was no concrete news of people or individual villages which kept women in the uncertainty.

For the sea travel local Chadians had put them in contact with the captain of a ship with Liberian flag, which was departing towards Marseille in two days, as soon it completed its load of cotton fiber; the freighter had two cabins for passengers, who were free. The captain named Sarckys was a sullen subject, but Chadians reputed him as reliable.

Once arrived in Marseille, they crossed the migration area without problems, since the three women had French passports and had papers that proved the paternity of Hubert. As for Cristian he held his Argentine passport with a French visa obtained at the Consulate in N'Djamena.

During the stay for a couple of days in Marseille they were contacted by members of their ethnic group resident in Paris, which got them accommodation in the French capital.

While Souady and Charfadine remained with the child in the hotel, Fatima and Cristian went to the small office that Chadians had rented.

There the director of the place, which was a mixture of commercial office with the Central Africa refugee centre, introduced himself ceremoniously.

"I am Monsieur Yannick, I have had the honor to meet your father Chief Ousmar Djalali and we have had frequent contacts and even trade." He paused while a beautiful African employee served coffee. "I have already put my contacts in our homeland -or what remains of those contacts- in search of news about Mr. Djalali and your village. The current situation in Central Chad is very unclear and we know that there are masses of refugees moving in all directions, towards Niger, Nigeria, Cameroon, the Central African Republic and Sudan. Apparently they are hundreds of thousands of people and it wills a take long time to get lists with names and when we get them they are likely to be incomplete." He stopped and handed to Fatima a block of paper and a pen. "Please let me have a list with the names of the persons that of particular interest to you in order to track them as a priority. Please come and see me again in four days. Anyway, just in case there is any news before let me have the telephone number of your hotel and I'll call you."

Once accomplished their task, Fatima and Cristian went out to explore the nearby quarter of Montmartre. As soon as they started walking, the romantic *ambiance* of the neighborhood engulfed them while they roamed its wavy streets, populated by Bohemian Paris dwellers and indeed global visitors. They stood in one the posts of street performers, and Cristian asked one of them to perform a more than acceptable portrait of his wife. They stopped at one of the sidewalks *cafes* and sat on a table, from where they observed the passage of pedestrians, some busy and others strolling, including many tourists.

Concerns that had chagrined them in recent weeks yielded momentarily to a feeling of *bonheur*. They were well aware that when returning to their hotel their reality would be present again, but their nervous systems and their souls desperately needed that haven to go ahead.

"There is no city in the world comparable with Paris." Exclaimed indeed Fatima, overcoming for a moment the tension that had invaded her body and mind after their haphazard escape from Chad. "Not even New York, nor by far."

Cristian, who had not been before in the city was delighted with this tour inadvertently intercalated in their escape plan. Hand in hand they wandered aimlessly through the area as two boyfriends until the shadows began to fall, and Fatima recalled that she had to feed Hubert.

Up the time limit set by him Fatima, Souady and Charfadine attended the pompous *Monsieur* Yannick Office to check if he had obtained news of relatives and friends, through his informal channels of Chadian exiles. They left the small Hubert at the care of the father who took him to a short walk in the vicinity of the hotel. When he returned the women had not returned yet.

At the end of one and half hours Cristian heard noises in the hall and soon distinguished the voice of her mother-in-law. He ran forward to open the door, and their faces prepared him for what was to come.

"Ousmar...?" He managed to ask.

"My husband is alive." Souady replied immediately "But has lost a hand in combat, by the explosion of a grenade. Apparently he also has scars all over his body."

"Haroun?"

Fatima hugged him strongly while she whispered.

"Your friend has died, *mon cher*." The woman felt the sharp contraction in all the muscles of Cristian. Charfadine also took him by the hand. A few whimpers emerged from the man throat. Who had been his companion, guide and confident in his random pass through territory African had died.

"How was it...?"

"As a hero." Replied Fatima "He stayed with a contingent of his men in the village to allow villagers to evacuate it, gaining precious time which allowed the majority to be safe. All of them fell."

Charfadine still was holding his hand. For the first time she spoke.

"If you had been there you would have fallen with them, and you would not have been able to put us safe." Looking him in the eyes she added "Don't you blame yourself? You couldn't have saved them."

"Africa is a very cruel continent with its children." Said somberly Souady.

As he saw his parents grieving gesture Hubert broke into tears, so Fatima set to calm him down.

"I never want to go back to my country." Whispered Charfadine so that only Cristian could hear her. "I can't stand the things happening there."

It was once again Fatima who attended to comfort his sister. Souady, who knew that in reality it was her function to contain her young smiled and with a firm voice said to her eldest daughter.

"Thanks to the gods that we have you at this terrible time. You're our rock and our oasis, our light in the wilderness."

"Night is never darker than before dawn." Replied Fatima "We will leave these trials strengthened."

"And how are things now?" Asked Cristian.

"It seems that the clan Mbaye stood up to circumstances. They sent their men to contain the aggressors and received our people and many more on their lands, which are now overpopulated." Replied Souady. "No doubt that my husband was right in not alienating their boss on the issue of Charfadine´s marriage. The ruse worked."

"My marriage a ruse?" Said Charfadine in a sad air of protest.

"The circumstances surrounding your marriage were actually a ruse to let you marry the man you love." Was her mother´s convincing response.

"And what else do you know?" Insisted Cristian.

"The French have put pressure on the Chadian Government to attack the aggressors in their rear, and it is said that planes have bombed them furtively, so the invasion is losing momentum and they hope to dislodge them from the sites they have occupied."

"I trust that in the coming days we can re-establish contact with my father." Expressed Fatima, hope that paradoxically tore off tears of her mother.

Souady brought together her daughters and her son-in-law and all merged into a hug, whose meaning escaped their understanding probably because it was actually addressed to their souls.

Indeed, the following week the go all went to M. Yannick´s office to talk by radio with Ousmar. The old warrior´s broken voice spoke clear enough of the emotion he was under. Souady spoke first.

"Ousmar Djalali." Said the matron once that both could overcome the invasion of feelings. "My place is with you, and I want to go back. No matter what dangers the future will bring we´ll face them together."

"I understand and I feel the same, but it is not yet the time. We are installed in very precariously in Mbaye territory. I believe that soon we will return to our lands, although perhaps not yet to our village. When this happens, I will call you by my side."

Fatima spoke in second place. Her father was very interested in the health and growth of his grandchild so she gave all kinds of details in this regard. He finally told her.

"Fatima. There is nothing that I want more than to see my daughters and my grandson. But this country will be dangerous for a long time and I do not expose our future. Follow your husband on the way he chooses and also you'll get back when the situation is mature."

The next round was Charfadine´s, who was constantly interrupted by tears. Ousmar did not know it, but it was the girl´s farewell to her past in Africa. In fact, the only one who could reveal the meaning of that conversation was Cristian.

Finally, the old Chief asked to speak to his son-in-law, who was also visibly affected by emotion.

"Cristian." He told "All that I care in the world is in your hands now, and I trust them." He made a halt to recompose the breath. "Tell me; are you free to return to your country?"

"Of course, I don't have pending accounts anywhere."

"Then take my daughters and grandson with you. They deserve a life of tranquility. Educate well your son, who someday will have high responsibilities. Providing time I will call Fatima and Hubert with me. Charfadine and you will be free to choose your destiny. You will be welcome in our land any time."

"I won´t let you down Chief Djalali. If I may I'm going to make a request."

"Tell me."

"Take care of Haroun´s wives and children."

"No doubt I will. He is the hero of our people."

Souady said goodbye once more and then the communication ended after three months of uncertainty and despair.

CHAPTER 15

The Charles De Gaulle airport was extremely busy at that time in the morning. People of all ethnic origins, nationalities and outfits filled lobbies paying attention to the screens which reported departures and arrivals. Sitting near a gate where the Air France flight to Buenos Aires had already been announced and which would depart in an hour, Souady, her two daughters, her son-in-law and grandson passed their last moments together until an uncertain fate brought them together again, none of them knew when or where. Souady held Hubert on her lap, asleep despite the uproar around them. Fatima and Charfadine surrounded her with her arms, while Cristian walked up and down anxious as before every trip by plane. The matron was inexplicably happy. The latest news from her husband in Chad predicted a return to the village sooner than anticipated, and the family around her filled her desires. The expectation of staying alone in Paris for a time did not worry her at all since she would always be and contact with M. Yannick and their peers. She knew that Fatima and her grandson would return to the village when the guarantees were given, but deep at her heart Souady wondered if she would see Charfadine again, her favorite daughter, and her little girl. She shook her head to chase away gloomy thoughts, and said to herself: you can always go to visit her to Buenos Aires or wherever she is. The Djalali family was not poor and could afford her journey.

Taking charge of her mother´s situation Fatima approached her and said.

"Let me know as soon we can go, even to visit you. And if your return to Chad is delayed we will have prepared a place for you wherever we are.

"What are the plans as you arrive?" Souady asked addressing Cristian.

"My brother and my brother-in-law will come and get us to the Ezeiza airport in Buenos Aires. We will travel directly on the same day to my hometown, Venado Tuerto, in the Province of Santa Fe. There we are staying at my parent's house, which is very broad, especially now that their four children have married and live on their own. With time I plan to find a house and a job in Buenos Aires, which is a very large international city."

At that moment the speakers gave boarding instructions and passengers began form a row to get into the plane. Charfadine, who had remained silent tightly, hugged her mother with tears in her eyes.

"Do not be afraid, *ma petite fille*, your mother will seek you and will find you wherever you are.

The aerial view of the city of Buenos Aires hit Fatima that had in mind a certain image of a Latin American city and met with a vast and modern metropolis of rational design. Charfadine watched the country that received her with great anxiety but in silence. Cristian was trying to describe them what was to be seen from the air but could barely beat a lump in the throat by returning to his homeland.

Gonzalo, the elder brother turned out to be a young sympathetic and expansive man, with air of family with Cristian, but dark hair and eyes. He was dressed in jeans, a sport jacket and slippers. Eduardo, Cristian's brother-in-law was a bit older and kept to himself. Cristian warmly greeted their relatives, whom he had not seen in the past four years. Both men had traveled from Venado Tuerto with two trucks of double cab and cargo box, stained externally with mud, clear sign of agricultural use to which they were applied. The interiors of the cabins were however ample and clean. Cristian, Fatima and Hubert traveled with Gonzalo, while Charfadine went with Eduardo.

The first contact with his brother-in-law was extremely pleasant to Fatima, despite the language limitations. Gonzalo could barely speak

English and a bit of French so Cristian translated the rest. Hubert looked out of the window absorbing the landscape in silence.

When they left the city and began to pass through suburban areas, the woman was impacted this time by the dimensions of the so-called Greater Buenos Aires, including some slums also of large dimensions. Later cityscape gave way to the rural, with large areas devoted to agricultural work. Cristian could not feel a certain pride to show his country to his family.

Charfadine looked at the agrarian scene with singular pleasure. Although she had also lived in France she only knew the capital city and parts of the countryside, very different from the extent that now opened before her eyes. Eduardo, who did not speak another language than the Castilian, overcoming his natural timidity indicated her certain sites and gave their names, which she couldn't remember but appreciated the gesture of hospitality of the man. As the van devoured miles it was growing inside her an overwhelming conviction that this was the place where she wanted to live. Charfadine, a sensitive spirit, had barely overcome all the sufferings and the physical and emotional instability of the last months and wanted desperately to turn page and find her place in the world. The Argentine prairie- as had done earlier with many newcomers - showed her its smiling face.

Arriving at Venado Tuerto the trucks did not enter the city but took a dirt road that forked from the route and drove a couple of miles along it.

" It´s not only dust, but what we call an "enhanced" road." Told Cristian to Fatima.

"And what is the difference?

"That is passable with a moderate rainfall, and depending on who drives, even with a torrential rain."

Torrential rains in the countryside were outside the universe of experiences of Fatima, however the periods spent in the United States and France.

At last they came to a large chalet-style house located beside the road, access to which was through a casuarinas grove that whistled at a gentle breeze blowing across them. The whole wide field, whose boundaries were lost on both sides was surrounded by a fence, and the entrance was through a *tranquera*, simple gate that was opened simply by removing a simple lock and whose only purpose was impeding the passage of animals.

Luis Colombo and his wife Graciela were already at the door of the chalet, expectant to receive their son after his prolonged absence, and to meet their new relatives. Graciela ran to embrace Cristian with her face ravaged by tears, and it took a couple of minutes until he could articulate a word. Luis waited for his wife to give rein to their emotions and then shook to Cristian strongly.

"You're welcome, son." Simple said in a broken voice.

"Let me introduce my wife Fatima." Said the newly arrived when he was able to recompose. "And this is Hubert, the grandson that you still never met."

Fatima was expectant of any hint of backlash by his in-laws faced with a color daughter-in-law, but found only smiles, and was surprised to receive a kiss of the woman kiss and a hug from the burly farmer, whom one minute before she did not know.

At the time arrived Eduardo's pick-up of and descended Charfadine who was wearing her blue robe on the travel clothes, and covered her hair with a kerchief of the same color. The visual impact of the exotic beauty was deep, and left her in-laws out of breath. Gonzalo, who had already had the same reaction at the airport broke his palms exclaiming festive.

"Well, let's see if someone helps me to get the baggage from the box of the truck. I wonder what they have brought from Africa that weighs so much!"

The Colombo had prepared for his son and his family a small house that was within the premises of the farm, and that was vacant since the children had become independent. As Cristian had announced his return from Paris more than one month in advance they had been able to refurbish it, and they had already moved the belongings that the young man had left when he traveled abroad. A small living room, it was a house of three bedrooms "one for each child" a wide kitchen and two bathrooms. The building dated back to about fifty years before but it was solid and in good condition.

"Almost custom made for us." Reflected Fatima.

"Choose a room for each one of you." Said Cristian. "I will leave my stuff in the smallest, that was precisely the one I had when I was a child."

That night they dined at the home the food that Graciela had prepared for them. They were exhausted by the long journey and the child was very excited.

"Tomorrow I have prepared a dinner in your honor at the big house, so you will know the rest of the family, at least those who live in Venado Tuerto." Told Graciela to Charfadine in her imperfect high school English.

The girl despite her somewhat insecure nature noticed that her mother-in-law was very pleased with her though she had not done much to deserve it so far. She was intrigued for the fact that those farmers welcomed a son who had been absent for his own will and who was returning in a situation of bigamy, married to two women of different race and different culture. Of her education in a religious school in France she recalled the parable of the prodigal son, which in this case had spread to his entire family. She drew the conclusion that her new family had a tradition of hospitality similar to that in force in sub-Saharan Africa rather than that of their European ancestors that Charfadine knew very well.

Charfadine stretched on the bed without undressing with the only purpose to enjoy her new situation, free of uncertainties and fears.

Then, under a rediscovered sense of well-being after a long period of stress she fell asleep.

On the following night all family members attended at the meeting, including Eduardo and his wife Monica with her three children and Gonzalo and his partner Sofia, with two sons, as well as several aunts and cousins. The Colombo had arranged the 'big house' for the event and they were wearing their Sunday clothes. The large table in the dining room was crowded of dishes and drinks, served on table cloths that were only occasionally used. The dishware was surviving pieces corresponding to several different sets.

The last to arrive were Fatima, Charfadine, Cristian and the small Hubert in his father's arms. Fatima was dressed in magnificent African attire, consisting of a dress from head to toe in apple green silk fabric, leaving only her face exposed. On top of it a wide bright red cape, lined with a green cloth a bit darker than the clothing she wore and a multi-colored kerchief covering her chest.

Charfadine wore also typically African clothing that mixed blue and violet colors. Both women provided a note of color and luster to a meeting where predominated the cold tones. Some local ladies were somewhat surprised at first, but the festive tone carried away all negative feelings.

Cristian raised his son in the air and said in a loud voice.

"Let me introduce the youngest of the Colombo. Next month he will be one year old.

He then went on to greet relatives who he had not yet seen, and he was greeted warmly and congratulated by his family. Rodrigo, one of the sons of Eduardo, two years old, touched his new cousin on the cheek surprised by its dark color, and immediately began to laugh as he hugged the small head. Hubert, infected of the mood, also began to laugh while he shook his little hands.

Fatima was aware of the aesthetic impact that she had produced, and moved with her usual fluency in social environments. She was soon surrounded by relatives who were trying to make themselves understood in English learned at school, or in French learned at home.

Graciela approached Charfadine and introduced her to each concurrent. The young woman with her calm attitude communicated with simplicity and sympathy with the new members of her extended family, while perceived the reactions of admiration and envy produced by her graceful movements. She had become aware that somehow her mother-in-law had decided to put her under her protection, which was understandably reassuring in this strange rural environment.

Fatima returned to her new home extremely pleased. She had confirmed that her natural charm and distinction had the same effect in this far South American atmosphere in some ways so strange, that in New York, Paris or her native village. She had undoubtedly been in the spotlight of Cristian's family that she accurately imagined representative of the rural middle class in the country. His son had been accepted as one Colombo, although she had plans for him. The skin color did not seem to be a negative factor, at least in their case.

Also Charfadine tried to evaluate her sensations and perceptions as she returned to her room. She knew that her sister had dazzled everybody by her exotic type and her social gifts, but she, Charfadine had no doubt stood out by her beauty; she had indeed felt in its silhouette all male eyes observing her askance.

The role that Graciela had assigned herself filled equally the void produced by the spatial distance of her biological mother. Charfadine still needed that female role in her life.

Finally, Cristian was also making a balance of the night. Definitely his maximum objective was fulfilled that night. His family had accepted so far his two wives and his son, so different and coming from so far. Possible issues arising from race or culture, and the fact of being bigamous had been buried and limited to predictable gossip that would last some time.

Fatima asserted that night her right as first wife and dragged Cristian to her bed. While she wrapped her long legs around him she told him.

"You peasant, make love to your Lady with all your strength."

CHAPTER 16

Six months had elapsed since the arrival of the family in Venado Tuerto; Fatima and Charfadine had already acquired a certain rudimentary handling of the language were managing their house. Hubert had completed his first year and was in the permanent company of his cousins which predicted a happy childhood. Cristian collaborated with rural chores in the family farm, which meant making long and intense workdays, interrupted by frequent rains, sometimes torrential which appropriately fecundated the so-called *pampa húmeda*, part of the best agricultural land in the country and the planet.

Fatima was in intermittent contact with Chad, and had spoken to Souady the day prior to her departure from Paris for N'Djamena, where she could at last get together with her husband. After the last and laborious communication she discreetly met Cristian who was returning from his work in the fields. When she told him that she needed to talk with him it did not surprise him, since he had somehow noticed the process his wife was undergoing.

"Today I have spoken directly with my father. The Government has appointed him within a Committee composed of officials, politicians and tribal leaders who are designing the new Chad, after the recent civil war and the infinite series of coups and revolutions." The woman took a brief respite before continuing. "They have appointed members of several delegations abroad that will have mission of getting international political, financial and commercial support for this process. I've been nominated within one of these offices in the Americas, by my personal knowledge of the exiles during the years that

I've been working with them, and my performance in the diplomatic areas."

As she saw her husband frown she added.

"It is a crucial stage in my country and I cannot skimp my effort, only because of family reasons."

"Only because of family reasons? Only for your family?" Reproached bitterly Cristian.

"You know how happy I've been here with yours, but it is a decisive stage in my life, that I don't want to see truncated."

"We are also are part of your life."

"And I absolutely want to include you at this stage. That why I'm talking to you, to see how we can reconcile career and family."

"What do you propose?"

"I need us to move to Buenos Aires. Although in this country there is not a large African community, there are embassies and consulates, and the means of communication and transportation that I need."

"Transport. What do you mean?"

"I will have to travel with a certain frequency to United States, Europe, and also occasionally to Chad."

The discussion stopped being purely discursive and Fatima began to use the means of persuasion that always gave her such good results with her husband, who ended up giving his consent to the requirements of his wife. She only asked him to convince Charfadine and anticipated that it would not be an easy task, because the girl had integrated very quickly to her new environment and was reluctant to everything which would bring instability.

Cristian had returned from Buenos Aires, where he had rented a small apartment with three bedrooms in a middle class neighborhood, quite crowded but well connected. Gonzalo and Eduardo offered once again to move the family of four people and their belongings, which had increased considerably in the months they lived in Venado Tuerto.

Fatima was exultant by returning to a large city with an offer of goods and services of international level, and access to international contacts that her new semi-official role imposed her. Charfadine instead knew in advance that she would miss the quiet town that he had enjoyed in their rural chapter, and above all the support and containment she had found in the Colombo family, notably in her mother-in-law, who promised to visit his son often anyway.

Two days after arriving in Buenos Aires Fatima received an instruction to attend a meeting of migrants from various African countries in Sao Paulo, Brazil. By the busy nature of the agenda she could not take the small Hubert with her so he was left with his father and aunt in Buenos Aires. Charfadine looked after him with patience and it was evident that the child was joyful in her company.

Cristian had gotten a job as a graphic designer and was away from home from seven in the morning until seven in the evening, when he returned exhausted. Charfadine already had bathed, changed and fed her nephew, who was often asleep upon the return of his father.

One night he returned and Hubert was still awake. Charfadine tried to give him in his arms, but the creature clung to his aunt, reluctant to go with his father. Cristian took note of mutual dependence that both had reached, which left him in meditation.

That night, Cristian slid into the bed of Charfadine, who was asleep. He kissed her gently on the cheeks and lips, until the girl woke up smiling. He then began a downward trajectory that took him to the long neck and perfect shoulders while she responded complacent but passive. When he stroked and kissed her breasts she issued sweet sounds while she caressed his head and messed up his hair. As he descended to the belly it began to oscillate up and down out of pleasure, which increased when he licked her Mount of Venus. Then he slid his hands by the inner side of her thighs and kissed them. She caught his head between her thighs and pressed it forcefully, took it with her hands and pushed it inside of her. Cristian understood the message and began to practice the oral sex. The girl began shaking frantically on the bed until she eventually reached the climax in a rattle. Cristian was really surprised by the intensity of the response to his efforts which filled him with excitement. He introduced himself inside her and until they arrived, this time together, at the Summit of pleasure.

Exhausted, they slept embraced until dawn, aroused by the cries of Hubert. When Charfadine returned after taking care of the child Cristian was sitting on the bed.

"Well?" She asked.

"Well what?"

"What did you think?"

"Exquisite, we have never had a night like that. And what do you think?"

"Better than on our wedding night."

"Why?"

"Well, I was then a virgin, I was tense, had confused feelings and fear to not to be up to the occasion. However last night it has been total release."

"It should be, since I am your husband."

"And yet I am always afraid."

"Afraid of what?"

"Of the comparison."

"Comparison with Fatima?"

"Yes."

"Forget the comparisons. You are you, and you are a woman with everything you need to make happy a man, not only physically but in your instincts. You're not inferior to anyone."

He took her tenderly in his arms and they stood together silently for a long time. Charfadine was processing and slowly tasting everything that had happened and had been spoken, as a process of growth of her internal confidence was taking place.

In her introspection, the woman soon realized that the factor that had enabled her to behave sexually uninhibited as that night was Fatima's transient remoteness, perhaps due to her role of older sister, but more probably by being the first wife of Cristian, like someone who enjoys titles of rightful owner. Anyway, now that she had fully enjoyed a night with her husband, the young woman was not willing to go back. She would continue on the course started that night and expected things would accommodate around her. She wondered if all women married with polygamous husbands in state experienced the same internal process.

Cristian at the same time, although not with all the details, had noticed the change in Charfadine. He suspected that the reason was the same Charfadine had arrived at, and also came to the conclusion that once the shell was broken there would be no turning back. Given Fatima's strong character he prayed the new situation would not bring internal conflict in his family. Indeed, since their arrival in Argentina Cristian was living in the best of all possible worlds.

Taking advantage of the bright morning of that Sunday they had gone for a walk at the Rivadavia Park, close to their apartment. They carried Hubert in a stroller, but the soil covered with lawn allowed him to walk with his uncertain steps and his constant falls; immediately two other children of similar age joined in their games. Cristian took Charfadine's hand walked a short distance, always keeping the child at sight.

For her, the experience was both new and stimulating; the perfect weather, a nice place full of couples both young and mature, children of all ages running, walking, biking or skating, they could feel free in an open space not too crowded. Charfadine deeply inhaled the warm air.

"Buenos Aires does honor to its name." She finally said.

"At this moment." Responded Cristian with his usual objectivity devoid of romanticism. "But there are often storms causing flooding, intense heat in summer and quite cold weather in winter. The stations are well marked here."

"But it's a city in which I would like to live. It has all kinds of activities."

"I will take it into account." He said smiling.

"But it may not always be suitable for Fatima's activities." Charfadine unexpected sentence of had a hint of resignation, as if a cloud suddenly covered the blue sky.

"It may be so." Replied sadly the man.

Walking back Cristian's cell phone rang.

"It is a message of Fatima."Said." She returns tomorrow at 6 pm Buenos Aires time."

Charfadine involuntarily tightened him arm what didn't go unnoticed. A few minutes later they entered the building and their apartment. Hubert had slept in his stroller during the return journey, so they put him in his bed.

Suddenly Charfadine took her husband's arm and led him to her bedroom he pushed him on the bed with some violence and began to undress hastily. Then she threw herself upon him with an unexpected passion.

"Well." said smilingly Cristian. "Every day a surprise."

"Shut your mouth and make me love!"

Cristian was waiting at the airport the arrival of Fatima's flight. He had bought a small second hand car. The ten days period that she scheduled to be in Sao Paulo had extended to almost a month due to meetings with influential personalities who had traveled to Brazil, so the woman was eager to be with her family again.

As they arrived at the apartment Charfadine opened the door still carrying Hubert in her arms after changing him. The sisters kissed and Fatima extended her arms to take her son in them, but the child moved away violently clinging to her aunt.

"But, Hubert, it's *Maman*." exclaimed embarrassed Charfadine. "Go with her!"

"Okay "said Fatima with resignation. " Do not force him. He has lost the habit of seeing me and now must familiarize with me again."

"Indeed in all this time also I have almost lost the habit of seeing you." Scolded with feigned anger Cristian who entered in the apartment again loaded with luggage. "I see you bring back a lot more stuff than you took to Sao Paulo."

"Of course! I had to buy more clothes in Sao Paulo to extend the stay."

Finally the child agreed to pass into the arms of his mother, who kissed him affectionately on the forehead. Charfadine helped Cristian to locate the suitcases, and Fatima noticed an almost imperceptible friction between their bodies, which was innovative. The manners of her sister with the man were more natural, less repressed than what Fatima remembered.

"Well, not only the child has established a close relationship with his aunt." Thought the traveler.

After talking for quite a while all three, basically about Fatima's experiences in Brazil and the progress of Hubert as far as walking and acquiring a rudimentary language, that lay on the bed to rest a bit before taking a shower.

Reflections came to Fatima's mind in droves. She was sure that her sister and her husband had established relations of a different nature than they had before her departure. These were probably not only of a sexual nature but also a greater level of intimacy. This was actually predictable and they could not be blamed for that since they were also husband and wife.

Fatima had chosen a course for her own life that had led her to be a kind of Stateswoman, although she preferred to use terms related to loyalty to her family and ethnicity and devotion by her father. In that course there were prices to be paid. Instead of staying to live comfortably in New York with the man she loved, her star had pushed her to return to her country, marry and give birth in it for not only familiar but also dynastic reasons. Thereafter she had not only accepted but proposed sharing her man with another woman, even if she was her sister, also for State reasons, and events had dragged everyone to this new country where Charfadine no doubt had taken roots. Fatima could not complain because at the bottom of everything was always her performance. But now she would fight to regain her role, her entire role.

CHAPTER 17

When Cristian returned home it was almost eight o'clock. He was physically and mentally tired. In the new post he had obtained in the publishing house it was clear that his employers would not simply give him the salary as a present, but he had to struggle to earn it and he was going to defend his position with tooth and nail. He had never had before a position of responsibility as the current. It involved a certain social life that Cristian didn't care much about, but he had to recognize that attending meetings of editors and writers with Fatima gave him an enhanced visibility since his wife became naturally and spontaneously in one focus of attention. While his Spanish was still incipient, she expressed herself in a grammatically correctly way, and her marked French accent was normally well accepted by the most diverse interlocutors.

It had passed already a year and half since their arrival in the city, and this period had been prodigal in events. Hubert went to a maternal garden where he was very well adapted, Charfadine had validated the degrees obtained in France and begun studies of human nutrition in the Faculty of Medicine of the University of Buenos Aires, and Cristian had escalated in the editorial thanks to his ample range of criteria to approaching a problem, fruit of a varied life experience and undoubtedly the endowments of natural intelligence.

Fatima had added to her diplomatic functions the management of funds of the Sara ethnic group abroad, and had to travel regularly. Souady had arrived a fortnight before in Buenos Aires to share the life of her daughters and her grandson, even at the expense of leaving her husband in the midst of difficulties and challenges of all kinds. The conflict between the role of mother and wife had been temporarily settled in favor of the first.

The political situation in Chad was stabilizing, and now the center of the conflict had moved to neighboring Central African Republic, with similar contours of racial and political hatreds, and similar military involvement of France and other European countries in the lid.

Cristian had bought an old but comfortable house in the neighborhood of Villa Urquiza, and although all had longer journeys to their activities, housing offering comforts for its breadth, which had allowed them to accommodate Souady. It was also more appropriate conditions for the breeding of the small Hubert, who already moved by his own means.

Upon entering the house Souady received him precisely with Hubert in her arms. In a music center sounded an old recording of *Vous lui direz* song by Mireille Mathieu.

"Souady." Said Cristian with an impatient gesture. "I already told you that the child already walks perfectly. You must not get him used to be in the arms of adults again. When you return to Africa we have no way to keep him happy."

"That's what we grandmothers are for, to spoil our grandkids." She challenging replied. However she left the boy on the ground, which ran out chasing a ball.

"Don't forget that Hubert is the only grandchild I have so far, when you should have given me at least three with my two daughters."

"Not everyone has to move with your tribal codes."

"And what codes have you instead? Those of this city, where half of the population live alone? Full of divorced, separated, coupled, and separated again people."

In his relations with the women of the clan Djalali, Cristian had learned that he ran with handicap, and that always there was a traditional way to see things that ultimately became irrefutable. So he changed the axis of the discussion.

"In fact, if you want more grandchildren you should convince Fatima not to travel so much."

"And what about Charfadine?"

"She must not discontinue her studies. She has a long time ahead."

"Does it mean that they are avoiding it?"

"For the moment, Yes."

Souady shook her head. She was not convinced that giving her grandchildren was responsibility of just one of her daughters. In addition, she yearned to have a grandchild of her favorite daughter.

"Certainly I'd like to talk to Fatima to stay more with her family but then I would have to fight with my husband." Added Souady. "The fact is that my daughter has become indispensable to get our people the necessary outside support. What you are experiencing are the problems of success, not of failure."

"That's not much comfort to me. By the way, do you know why she has not arrived yet?"

"She was retained downtown by a meeting with foreign financiers that are in the city. And Charfadine? I am concerned that she comes so late".

Typical Souady and her penchant for her youngest daughter. What was explainable in Fatima was a source of concern in the case of Charfadine.

"She has practical works. It ends at nine pm." Replied resignedly Cristian.

Then the sound of keys in the door of the House was heard and Fatima entered.

"Pouf!." Growled "The subway was so crowded that I had to miss three formations before I could climb and travel standing. More travel frequencies are necessary."

She left her purse on the table and threw her shoes in anger. Cristian ceded the first turn of the shower while playing with his son on the floor.

When he left the bathroom found had also Charfadine had arrived with similar complaints about the means of transport.

"When we went away from Chad you didn't tell us about transportation problems in Buenos Aires, otherwise I would not have come." Exaggerated.

"That is a sign of good integration to the country and its customs." said the man "Complaining about everything."

After dinner and bedtime to Hubert, the four adults gathered for a coffee.

Fatima narrated the negotiations with financiers.

"The main difficulty to obtain financing for African countries is the inter-ethnic tension, which explodes with any excuse." She explained.

"Which largely comes from the boundaries drawn with a pencil by the colonial powers of the time." Cristian said.

"Yes, it's true, but there has been time long enough since independence to settle the problems in an unbloody manner" Sid his wife.

"Argentina's independence was declared in 1816, and only in 1852 some lasting peace was achieved. During the interregnum the warlords dominated the scenery." insisted he.

"That was in Century 19th. We are in the 21st. The world does not tolerate such remnants of the past any more. There is no alternative to negotiated solutions, even in Africa. There are cases of various Nations that coexist perfectly, as Switzerland, with four national languages and two religions."

"Yes, but countries highly civilized as Canada or Belgium have problems to handle the differences between their linguistic groups." He replied stubbornly.

"It is truth Cristian, but they do not settle their differences with ethnic cleansing."

"Note the cases of the former Soviet Union and Yugoslavia. And now it will restart in Ukraine."

"It is precisely my point. That is intolerable. We must settle differences, and if necessary change the borders to more realistic ones, but without bloodshed. No, the cliché of the colonial borders does not explain the current massacres, is looking to the past or blame foreigners to evade the current responsibilities, as you Argentineans love to do."

Cristian finally surrendered. He knew in advance that he could not beat his wife in an intellectual terrain, mostly in one she had worked so hard. To sum up the differences between both arguments were reduced to the glass half full or half empty issue and he did not want to appear as pessimistic or fatalist.

"I will have to travel to New York." Said Fatima after a brief silence "I have to attend a meeting of African countries at the United Nations."

"There is always some reason." Said bitterly Cristian "We have barely seen you in the last month."

"I want it to be different this time." Replied enigmatically the woman.

Aware of the expectation she had created, Fatima began to persuasively explain her intentions. The other three knew in advance that finally they would to yield, both by the ascendancy Fatima had as by the degree of elaboration that in general had her proposals.

"Taking advantage of the fact that *Maman* will be in Buenos Aires for another fifteen days and Charfadine is having winter holidays at the Faculty, I think both you and I can travel together." She said referring to Cristian. "I feel much nostalgia and a desire to relive the moments and places of the time in which we met."

Fatima continued reasoning with her usual consistency, and everyone understood that she had carefully planned every detail.

"Though I benefit in this plan, it does not look fair for your mother and your sister." Protested Cristian. "Leaving them with the burden and responsibility for the child and the house while we go on a sentimental ride."

"For me there is no problem." Said immediately Souady, while Charfadine remained silent. The man shook his head resignedly and tried to reach some compromise.

"I propose that at least the two you and Hubert carry out the plan which I had already talked about. It's go to the Córdoba hills, a classic site for winter holidays. It has a cold but healthy climate without so much moisture and of sunshine afternoons."

Clearly the silence meant consent.

"When would this be?" Asked Cristian "Indeed I have vacation time available in the editorial, but I must plan how to leave my work in progress to my colleagues. I can't be a burden for them either."

Finally decided that since Fatima had to be in New York in less than a week, she would travel alone and Cristian would join her one week later, when the diplomatic meetings have concluded. In this way the work needs of both were taken into account.

"Thank you for having us in mind." Whispered Charfadine to Cristian once the meeting was over. "I'm sure that I will love to leave Buenos Aires with this cold."

"Bah! I see it as a mere consolation. But I promise I will compensate you in the future."

Fatima had already departed heading to New York, and Souady, Charfadine and Hubert would be traveling to Cordoba in half a week. Cristian decided to spend the nights in the bedroom of his second wife, although the bed was narrow.

"Since the main wife departed, it's now the turn of the concubine." Said ironically but with a hint of bitterness Charfadine.

"You know that it is not so." Cristian turned into Spanish, in which his skills of conviction were better "but let's not waste time in recriminations."

He slipped his hands between the sheets and introduced them in her nightgown of the woman, patting her belly. The arguments once again gave way to hormones.

Cristian took the women and children to the bus terminal and waited until the vehicle that would take them to La Cumbre departed. Then he turned to his work to complete second last working day before leaving. He didn't want to acknowledge it himself, but the idea of reviving the idyll with Fatima in New York, times when everything was clear, straight and bright had excited him.

CHAPTER 18

Fatima and Cristian were fatigued. Malik had carried the man from the airport the previous night and after a day of tour and some shopping on Fifth Avenue they returned to the hotel laden with packages. After showering they went to have dinner in a nearby restaurant. Most of the New Yorkers had already eaten, so it was not difficult for them to get a table; Fatima noticed that after a year and a half living in Argentina their habits had changed, including the hour of dinner.

They returned to the hotel hand in hand, took an espresso in the coffee shop, and then went up to the room. There Fatima took his hand and said sweetly.

"Undress me slowly."

"You want to repeat our first night?

"No. That was a whirlpool, a hurricane. Let's leave it for another day. Now love me with care as befits a lady."

"To a Princess?" Cristian was mocking Malik.

"Yes. Is it that you have doubts?"

"No, none at all." As it was customary, he not could object to the arguments of his wife, shielded from her own logic. He began to unbutton her dress.

The next day they decided to continue their sentimental journey in the Gramercy Park area, where they had passed the second part of their stay in New York, under pressure from ethnic and political enemies of Fatima's father. They walked hand in hand along the elegant streets, sipped a coffee in one of its coffee shops, and then wandered in the libraries. They could not sit in the Park, whose entrance is forbidden to those who are not neighbors holding a key.

That afternoon, as the weather allowed it they decided to go to the Central Park, explore the extensive trails, sit and stroke each other in a bench discreetly covered from outside looks by small groves, and feeding small animals approaching them without fear. The state of reverie carried them to two years before, with its infatuation full of urgency, intensity and anxiety, feeling that had been partially extinguished with coexistence and troubles of life in the desert first, and in the city then, but whose embers were alive and ready to gain strength again when the circumstances were propitious. Fatima sighed happily with the feeling numb and now rediscovered.

That night they invited Malik to dinner at a good restaurant. The man appeared with his immense body contained in an elegant suit, with white shirt and tie to the tone of the costume.

Fatima was dressed in a sober somewhat Westernized tribal outfit, enhancing her magnificent figure. Cristian was as always with green wrinkled cotton trousers and a worn Brown faux leather jacket.

Since in previous days he had not been able to ask Fatima- by time pressure for her meetings and also by prudence- Malik was eager to know about the life of the couple since they had left New York. He congratulated them for their son, and if he was surprised to learn that Cristian had also married Charfadine- who he did not know personally, only by references- he hid it very well.

At that time Fatima asked by his wife and four daughters, one of which was preparing to enter the University of Columbia. When the subject turned to the political situation in Chad, Fatima summarized the latest developments, beyond what was published in the news media.

"Chad looks calmer now, although we know that supporters of Al-Qaida are on the lookout to rekindle the flame of ethnic conflict anytime. But they suffered many losses in the last internal war, of which did not recover. They are now also involved in the Central African

Republic, your homeland, and probably cannot keep so many fronts open at the same time."

Malik gave a brief description of the continuation of the struggles in New York after the couple had gone out. Although he avoided every gruesome detail, the lid had been bloody, and had not transcended only because it was masked in the gang wars. Before Fatima questions about old acquaintances, in some cases he should report that they had died. Others had instead returned to Africa due to the prospect of peace and economic improvement in certain areas.

Returning late to the hotel, the woman disrobed with certain brightness in her eyes that Cristian knew very well.

"Well, shall we continue in the slow and sweet wave?"

"None of that! After Central Park, I want now to reconnect with fire."

Souady, Charfadine and Hubert were waiting at the airport in Ezeiza, in Buenos Aires. Charfadine had premiered her new driver's license, in her eagerness to complete her Argentine documents, maybe an involuntary testimony of her mental integration to the country. Now Cristian was driving back home.

Returning the five on board with the suitcases put to the test the Ford cargo capacity, while he risked any possible objections from the police.

Fatima opened the suitcases but only took off them only the gifts brought for all, putting off the laborious time of extracting and accommodating her clothing and personal effects.

Hubert finally agreed to embrace his mother; This time the child initial reluctance of the child did not impacted Fatima, because it was discounted on the one hand, and her emotional state. Even for a person with a personality as strong and stable as her, the trip to the city where she had lived many years of her life and in particular the period she had spent with Cristian had a very high positive emotional impact.

The day in which Souady should return to his country finally arrived, since she missed her husband and had a number of long-postponed household chores and duties. Transfer to Ezeiza airport was again with the car full.

Souady walked with firm step towards the gate of access to the international area, without looking back to prevent breaking down. Hubert cried to see his recently recovered grandmother suddenly leave again.

The following days, the absence of Souady made feel with all intensity for all, especially for Charfadine and Hubert, who were those who had had a more solid connection with the matron.

Friday Cristian returned home a little earlier.

"How are you going with your studies?" He asked Charfadine.

The girl gave all kinds of explanations, which showed clearly her enthusiasm and expectations.

The talks between the two were long in Spanish due her insistence on the need to master the language, particularly for his studies in the Faculty, which required a fluid management and somewhat intimate of the language that she considered as well as the French subtle and elegant. Since she also unfolded friendships with peers of the Faculty, she gave importance to speaking the River Plate dialect spoken in Argentina.

"In short, you want to become one Argentine." Stated rather than asked Cristian.

"Except for the color of the skin."

"There is no "Argentine" skin color. That doesn't seem to bring you problems either. Don't believe that I don't see how men down the street watch you."

"Do not tell me that you're jealous."

"Should I be?"

Then Fatima joined them, asking about the subject of the conversation.

"I really feel the looks of men stuck on my butt. Worse than in France or Italy."

"Really difficult that your buttocks can go unnoticed here."

"That is because there are no black women."

"Boys traveling to Brazil sigh with the buttocks of the *mulatas*."

The talk had diverted its course for the taste of Charfadine, from the color of her skin to the back of her sister. She tried to then bring it back to safe ground.

"The next is a long weekend. Any plans?"

"We can go to the coast." Proposed Cristian.

"It is almost winter." Objected Charfadine. "What can we do in a beach resort?"

"Take a walk along the beach."

"There will be no one there." Replied Fatima.

"On the contrary. There are the winter school holidays. Many families migrate looking for new landscapes and getting out of the cities."

They rented two pieces at a hotel in a resort called Costa del Este, consisting of a series of blocks with houses of varied dimensions, not big but very attractive, with streets of pavement or sand and a small shopping centre. Pine trees and other tree species created everywhere a habitat not indigenous but very natural and healthy. There were few people, reason why the jeeps and ATVs drove at high speed through the winding streets. The hotel, was directly on the beach, so they barely accommodated their stuff in the closets and changed with sports clothing and got out to walk on the sand. Hubert ran on a completely unknown environment, stumbling and falling into the arena that was novel and surprising. Resins of pines and other fragrances created a cool environment.

When they were together the three adults spoke in French not to exclude Fatima whose Spanish was more basic than Charfadine´s, partly because she spent much less time in Buenos Aires due to her travels abroad.

"What a huge beach!" Exclaimed Charfadine. "I had never seen anything like this before."

"In low tides you have over a hundred meters wide." Cristian explained "And this extends to other beaches by miles and miles."

"And are the waters deep?" Asked Fatima.

"Yes, of course, is the Atlantic Ocean, but the decline is gradual, less abrupt than in Rio de Janeiro and Miami."

Hubert came trotting literally covered with sand and Fatima began to laugh.

"You will soon have chance to try the sand in Chad!"

A shiver ran through Cristian spine. He looked into Charfadine eyes and noticed that her reaction was similar. The theme was a thorn that could dig into their flesh at any time.

They toured hundreds of yards along the beach until the houses ended and beaches ended in high and endless dunes.

"Dunes like in Sahara!" "Said Fatima "this landscape is more familiar.

They sat down in the dunes to rest for a while, until the rays of the Sun started retreating from the beach.

"Better go back." Said Cristian." Hubert is already tired and I have to carry him in my arms."

When arrived at the hotel the shadows were already falling on the beach and the grove surrounding the building was a dark mass.

After dinner they stayed at the lobby where they rarely saw any delayed tourist or night hotel employee. They remained there long hours at the heat of a wood fire in a large hearth. Hubert fell asleep on his mother's lap, while the adults talked about the day's experiences. When the subject was exhausted, the weight of the conversation fell on Fatima, who with her contralto voice narrated her activities in New York, during the meetings of African countries.

".. .with all its weaknesses and greatness, there is growing conviction that the effort to rid Africa of its wars, plagues, famines and exiles must come from Africans themselves. Others will hardly place their consciousness above their interests. And this is true for Europeans, Americans, Russians and Chinese."

A silence followed her words.

"What, not interested in the topic?" Challenged Fatima.

"What can add from our small beings to the great mission that you have drawn?" Surprisingly said Charfadine without double intentions.

"There is no such grandiose mission! The task is for not an enlightened élite, but for everyone, at least those who are children of that continent."

"That excludes me "Cristian replied.

"Not! You have interests in this adventure. Two wives and a son, no less." Answered quiet but emphatically Fatima. "We have to earn the right to be proud of our continent as you are demonstrating these days to be it of your country."

"Country plagued by political, economic and social problems, all because of our transgressions, corruption and rebellions."

"But that is a haven for those arriving wounded, which opens up generously to those who arrive at its shores." Added Charfadine "I can attest it through my own experience."

The girl kept surprising her sister and husband with her interventions, which her usual low profile and discreet attitude did not allow to foresee.

The discussion ended and Cristian smiled; a debate of this kind it was not common in most households that he remembered. He stretched out on the couch under his son weight, closed his eyes and was carried away feeling how joy filled his senses. Fatima had brought a notebook to connect with the French newspapers on the Internet thanks to the hotel WiFi. From the device emerged the sound of *Ne me quitte pas*, song by Celine Dion.

Tout peut s'oublier
Qui s'enfuit déjà
Oublier le temps des malentendus
Et le temps perdu

CHAPTER 19

Fatima had been all afternoon working with her notebook and suffered from eyestrain. She had already been using lenses in the last six months to correct an incipient presbyopia. She leaned meditative over the back of the chair.

"Well, well. Let's see how do I tell them this?" She wondered. Her restless mind immediately began to evaluate alternative courses of action. She had already detected before in her the same signs of fatigue and the question came up ever more frequently.

"What would happen if I send all this to hell and dedicate myself to my family whose best years I am missing? I have everything to a woman of my age may want and I am always behind a mirage that recedes as I progress. My function gives me momentary satisfaction but deprives me of the maximum bonuses that my heart longs for. What if I say no? How would my father react? Who else could most play my role? How would my family work if I was present all the time? And finally, but only finally, how would I feel?"

She decided not to discuss with her husband and sister the contents of the e-mail that she had just received from the Ministry of Foreign Affairs and Cooperation of the Republic of Chad, until she had her own thoughts clear. The current Minister was her teacher and mentor during her studies in France and knew well her capacity and resolution. If she accepted it would not be a leap into the void, but the costs of an affirmative decision were predictable.

She heard that someone was opening the door; a quick glance at the clock told her that it was Cristian returning from his job. She closed the mail, shut off the computer and closed the lid to keep the problem away. She then got up and approached the door to greet her husband.

Hubert was already in front of the door pointing at it with the index finger while he mumbled.

"Dad.".

Fatima´s heart squeezed but she shook her head and forced a smile. At that time the man entered the house.

Cristian had already gone to work and Charfadine to the Faculty. Fatima had just finished changing Hubert, who had immediately gone to play in the small courtyard of their house, where his parents were convinced that there was no risk. The fixed telephone connected last week rang and its bell startled the woman, who rarely had heard it sound. Great was her surprise as she heard that at the other end was her mother Souady.

"*Oui, maman*, how are you? I see that you have received the message with my new phone number.

"And I prefer to call you to a regular phone, I don´t trust cell phones at all."

They were exchanging information on the status of the family in one and another side, and finally, Souady unveiled the true purpose of her call.

"*Ma chère fille*. The proposal that the Ministry of Foreign Affairs made you has reached my ears."

"I wonder how you know about it. It is assumed to be confidential and is also very recent."

"No matter how, the fact is that I learned. I hope your father will never hear about this call."

"Well, you've captured my attention. What is all this mystery about?"

"That I wish to give you my opinion... rather, my mother's plea."

"Go ahead."

"Declines the offer. Do not put your career before your family or you will make everybody unhappy."

A strong wave of uneasiness invaded Fatima, usually so self-confident, but her mother had touched a sensitive nerve that was aching from the day before.

The woman tried to calm her mother assuring her that she would do what she considered the best for the family, but without making specific commitments about her final decision. When they cut the communication Souady was more concerned than at the beginning.

The infighting that Fatima was going through deepened. Her mother involvement had highlighted the implications that her decision was to have for several people, precisely the ones she really cared about. By her training during long years she was used to act with determination in serious questions concerning her people, but in general the aspects in conflict were evident, the identity and interests of each party were crystal clear and also where the good for her people resided. But now there was a conflict, a clear contrast of needs and aspirations of her family, her ethnicity and her own, and inevitably to its decision, there would be winners and net losers among the people she loved. Even though she squeezed her brains there were no intermediate or compromise solutions that would leave all parties happy and all needs satisfied. She realized she was facing a trade-off, moreover, a dilemma.

For several days Fatima was irritable, sleepless and elusive. The others noticed it and adopted various reactions. Hubert cried more than usual, Charfadine usually attentive and friendly with her was now dodging her, and Cristian tried several times to gain her confidence in vain.

One of so many nights in white finally took his determination. She felt a twinge in her belly, but then it relented and she got finally sleep.

In the afternoon the next day, when everyone had returned to their duties, Fatima called a meeting by announcing that he had something important to communicate.

Hubert was asleep and all were sipping a cup of coffee. Finally Cristian said directly.

"Fatima, We are all awaiting your words. Please tell us what you have to say at once."

"Well, I will explain to you the dilemma I have facing in these days, and that, as all of you have noticed has eaten me internally."

She made a stop, sipped her coffee to clarify her voice and continued speaking without hesitation.

"The Minister of Foreign Affairs and Cooperation of Chad on behalf of the Government has made me an offer extremely attractive offer." She made another stop, choosing the words to continue, amid the absolute silence.

"It's the post of Deputy Minister in charge of International Economic Relations of the Republic of Chad."

Cristian choked and coughed, Charfadine looked down.

"It is the highest position ever achieved by a woman in Chad, or for that matter in the central region of Africa. Logically it is a position based in N'Djamena, but with many possibilities for trips."

The silence became deeper making it difficult for her to go on with her exposure.

"And well, what have you answered." Asked eventually Cristian.

"I have put as a condition to take all of you with me to N´Djamena. I have also asked -and am sure I will obtain it- a position in the same Ministry for you, Charfadine."

"But what was your decision?" Insisted Cristian in an unusually hard tone.

"Before communicating it to the Ministry I need to know your response to this offering to come with me."

Cristian stirred in his chair, took his head between his hands, and then looked at Charfadine. The situation did not require words; the girl had in her hands a decision which would have consequences for the whole family.

Charfadine raised her view and looked at sister and her husband with a firm gesture.

"I'm prepared to say what I will do. In reality I always knew that this situation would eventually occur, knowing Fatima's conditions your character. I have no doubt that Chad does not have a person more prepared than you for that position, to represent it throughout the world. I think that you cannot avoid following your star wherever it takes you."

Now it was her turn to make an ominous silence. Cristian followed her words with anguish on his face.

"But I also have the right to search my destiny and I firmly believe that it is in this country."

Cristian jump of his chair and silently began to make strides around the room, in order to balance tensions.

"For the first time I have my own place, not only for being someone's daughter or sister but for being myself in a large anonymous city where however I'm opening my space." Continued Charfadine "The fact that nobody here knows or cares who my father or my sister is paradoxically becomes an advantage. No one has previous expectations about me, except of course the two of you and no one is not willing to give me advantages. Whatever I achieve, I will achieve it on my own, it will be my success or my failure and no one can take it away from me. Colleagues and friends who have approached me do not know that my father is a mighty man, and do not even know where is Chad. And since they are actually a gang of nonconformists and mavericks it is better that they do not know."

Charfadine made a new pause; she swallowed aware that perhaps for the first time in his life now she was the center of attention, looked at Cristian's eyes and perceived a certain brightness that she interpreted as pride. But anyway it was no longer the others who determined her actions.

"I will not leave this country." She ended with a quiet voice and a serene gesture.

Cristian did not speak. He was actually the only one who was not prepared to take a stand. Although it was clear in recent days that Fatima was incubating an important and difficult decision the young man had forced the issue out of his head, because of the excessive tension that caused him considering the possibilities.

Now the options were clear. It was a partition of waters, the two women he loved were taking different paths in their lives and he had to decide which of these diverging rivers he would follow. There was no way to postpone the issue any more.

Surprisingly, and as had happened before in his life, just by obtaining clarity on the alternatives the decision arose spontaneously in his mind. He stood up before the inquisitive eyes of Fatima and Charfadine and left the room in silence, with a hint of bitter taste in his mouth but with peace in the soul.

CHAPTER 20

Fatima began the preparations to return to Chad a month after having taken her decision. She transferred the functions she carried out from Buenos Aires to another Chadian citizen living in Washington DC. She ensured that her contacts in the Ministry of Foreign Affairs and Cooperation would be responsible for renting her an apartment in N'Djamena and for enrolling Hubert in the kindergarten of a French school in the city. Her mother sent one of her maids of confidence to clean and condition the housing, and should Fatima and the maid agree to stay to live with her and attend the family in the city, given the tight agenda that her daughter would have once in office.

Cristian requested a leave without pay in his work and renewed his passport that was close to its expiry date; the visa issue was also resolved.

Means were provided to send money to Charfadine from Chad, so that she could advance in her studies without the immediate need to work. In spite of this, the girl began tutoring French in order to achieve her economic independence. The house would continue to be registered for the time being at Fatima's name until a final decision was taken, and the car was transferred to her sister.

When the time arrived Charfadine drove Fatima, Cristian and Hubert in auto to the Ezeiza Airport to take their flight to Paris.

While Fatima brought the boy to the bathroom to change his diapers, Charfadine and Cristian were alone in the waiting room Cristian gestured toward Fatima that already came out of the toilet. Charfadine approached her mouth to the ear of the man and whispered.

"I am pregnant."

Cristian did not utter a word, while his cheeks blushed as was his characteristic.

"Quickly! They are already calling to board "said Fatima in an urgent tone.

The three travelers headed to the area of international shipments. Fatima was carrying Hubert, while Cristian hauled two suitcases and several packages. When they walked through the glass door and he turned his view towards Charfadine. The young woman, leaning on a guardrail was watching to one side with an absent look. an intense fire swept the viscera of the man, consequence of his internal tearing.

When they arrived at the airport N'Djamena from Paris several dignitaries were expected them, including some uniformed. Immigration and customs formalities were overlooked, and within half an hour of arrival they were already aboard an official vehicle. They took them firstly to the hotel, where already Souady was waiting for them, excited about all the official protocol. There remained Cristian and Hubert, while Fatima was transported to a meeting with her friend the Minister and his *entourage*.

She returned at seven in the evening, tired and hungry. During dinner she narrated her experiences during her first official day, before the rapt gaze of her mother and the caring attention of her husband.

".. .And after tomorrow I will officially assume my position. The President and his wife will be present as well as all the Ministers. I'd like that you both could come. I think that I can get the necessary permission. Hubert can stay with the maid, who knows how to deal with children."

The huge official Hall of the Government Palace was filled with officials of Ministry of Foreign Affairs and Cooperation and other areas of the Central Government.

Fatima and her mother had reserved for the occasion their best ethnic attires; the future Deputy Minister was dazzling in broad layers that insinuating its silhouette.

The President was an imposing individual, about sixty-five years old, dressed in a Western outfit. The Minister for Foreign Affairs was about forty years old and had athletic appearance. He greeted Fatima with a formal kiss on each cheek; Cristian recalled that he had been her coach during her studies and had thus a long relationship.

Fatima swore vocalizing clearly despite the excitement that filled her. The President warmly greeted his new Deputy Minister, and as waiting for this gesture the crowd burst into applause. Despite his natural sobriety and detachment of pomp, a surge of pride also invaded Cristian, as Souady irrepressibly wept beside him.

After the formal ceremony a cocktail party was held in which Fatima had the usual brightness. Her manners, her attire and her beauty turned her into the central character of the evening.

Upon his return in the official car Souady did not stop pondering what happened.

"This is a milestone for all women in Chad and our ethnic group in particular. None of its members had ever reached to a position at national level. I hope that your father can enjoy the film they have recorded."

Ousmar could not be present at the event because it overlapped with an important meeting with the remaining heads of the Sara ethnic group.

"I hope that you can be in future events that surely will follow." Said confident Fatima.

"What most impacted me was the central role that you played at the cocktail." Confided Cristian. "You became the luminary of the night being that you really have just arrived."

"Fatima has an education, a personality and a bearing that none of these politicians can match." Replied Souady.

"You speak as if you were my mother." Said Fatima obviously pleased.

"In any case I am struck for the good reception you have received." "Insisted Cristian. "It does not match the image I have of the generosity of the politicians."

"What happens is that this country lacks natural leaders, and the Chadians are learning to recognize when one appears, even if it is a woman." Argued Souady.

"Maman, I think your interpretation is excessive."

"I guarantee it Fatima." Souady´s excitation of the mother had no limits. "This is only a first step in your political career."

The phrase was ringing in the head of Cristian. Despite it came from a maternal obvious enthusiasm, no doubt it had a good rationale. Fatima was projected in a race with a distant goal where the fences would be higher.

Two days later, Ousmar arrived at N'Djamena. He had traveled in a modern Mercedes Benz covered by the dust of the desert, but in good mood for having traveled enjoying the air conditioning.

When he saw his father-in-law arriving Cristian was surprised to remember the old and precarious vehicles he had seen during his stay in the village barely a year and a half before, including the one with which they had escaped from the invasion.

Before many witnesses of the event, Ousmar greeted his wife and his son-in-law in a rather cold and distant way, since he should preserve the authority associated with his current range. On the other hand was more effusive with his daughter and grandson, in view of her present status. His orthopedic hand could be hardly noticed and he used it naturally.

However, once in family, the Chief gave vent to his joy and had words of encouragement for all. Cristian meditated on the odd duties and limitations associated with the nature of a public person, hiding emotions even if they were burning the entrails. His personality rejected this aspect of power.

They were finally alone with Fatima and Hubert. The woman clung to his son and raised him despite his weight.

"It has been a glorious day for you. Is it not true?" Asked Cristian.

"It has been a very important day in truth, with a view to the future." Said the woman with a sad smile. "But it also gives a pattern on how that future will be."

"And how will it be?"

"Depersonalized. Pure representation."

"But you do not seem to dislike it. You have the conditions to succeed in it."

"There is always an opportunity cost. I am pleased with what I do, but it deprives me of other things that my soul cries out for."

"Then the lights, the shining colors and brightness of the position have not seduced you."

"I accept it as a liability and a burden. But we are done philosophizing. We haven't seen each other for almost a month.

She extended over his pants a long and slender leg, while taking between her hands one of his and slipping it on her thigh. Cristian felt a surge of excitement for his wife and rushed over her.

A week later the Djalalis returned to their village, including their daughter, grandson and son-in-law. The Princess and her first-born son ensured the future of the dynasty, and were at the top of their success. The reception was triumphant; the people that had recently emerged from the horrors of the civil war and were dedicated to a feverish reconstruction needed these signals of continuity and security and expressed their feelings in a clear and lively way.

Charfadine had dined alone as she returned from classes at the Faculty, and sat facing the computer as did every night before watching TV. She opened the mail and gave a leap when saw a CrisColombo message in the Inbox. Opened it eagerly and read the single line:

"I arrive Wednesday Air France 394 - Baires time 7:50. Do not-repeat do not- come to look for me."

The girl stroked her growing belly; needing to move to discharge adrenaline she stood up and looked involuntarily her image in the large closet mirror; then she saw her own serene and confident smile. Not for a moment she had doubted.

EPILOGUE

Charfadine waited the arrival of her husband with the dinner ready. The small Maxine was sleeping tired by the exercise of her first days in kindergarten. The woman heard the sound of the key in the lock and ran towards the door. Cristian looked tired from the days when you had to stay until eight in the evening in the editorial. He kissed her while he was pulling out his jacket and hung it on the rack. Then they disrobed and showered quickly, so symptoms of stress loosened whilst hose of tiredness exacerbated.

Charfadine had awakened the girl to dinner together and so that the father could see her at least once a day.

After dinner they kindled the TV, and going quickly through the local newscasts the woman set the French international channel, to see news that used to bring news of Africa.

After a long stretch dedicated to French internal politics the news from abroad commenced. The broadcaster reported a meeting in N′Djamena of the Foreign Affairs Ministers of the Sub-Saharan African countries to find a solution to the bloodshed in the Central African Republic. The image showed the opening speech of the Minister of Foreign Affairs and Cooperation of Chad as host of their peers.

"Watch." Said Charfadine to the little Maxine while pointing her index finger to the screen. That is aunt Fatima."

From the Author

D ear reader

I appreciate your interest in reading these few words in which I talk about my work. It is a good habit to try to understand what led an author to write a particular book, because the motivations vary from author to author and from book to book.

As a sign of respect for the reader, in all my books I make a thorough previous investigation of the facts the work refers to, particularly considering that many of them take place in places sometimes very far apart from each other and also in various historical periods; my books often travel indeed through dilated stretches in time and space.

These searches are based on my memory, in the large family library and the huge quarry of facts and data existing in the Internet. In the global network everyone can search but not all find the same ... fortunately, since this results in a huge variability and diversity.

The plot of course comes from the imagination and fantasy. This is critical for me and I confess that I would never write a book that I wouldn't like to read; my interests as a writer and as a reader coincide to a large degree.

My works often take place in exotic locations and refer sometimes to surprising and even paradoxical facts, but never enter the realm of the fantastic and incredible. Moreover, the most bizarre events are often true.

About the Author

C edric Daurio is the pen name an Argentine novelist uses for certain types of narrative, in general thrillers with esoteric or paranormal content. The author has lived in New York for years and now resides in Buenos Aires, his hometown. His style is clear and straightforward, and does not hesitate to tackle thorny issues.

Works by Cèdric Daurio

In English
Blood Runes
The Agartha Star
The Lost Legion
I Ching and Murder
Before the Storm
An Elegant Lady
South Wind
The Japanese Pianist
Templarii Australis

I
In Spanish
Runas de Sangre
La Estrella de Agartha
La Legión Perdida
Antes de la Tormenta
Una Dama Elegante
Viento Sur
I Ching y Crimen
La Pianista Japonesa
Templarii Australis

Coordinates of the Author

Mailto: cedricdaurio@gmail.com
Blog: https://cedricdauriobooks.wordpress.com/blog/

About the Publisher

Oscar Luis Rigiroli publishes the books in print and electronic editions through a commercial network that provides them with an ample worldwide coverage including sales in the five continents. The catalog includes titles of its own authorship as those written by other authors. All works are available in Spanish and English.

Abundant information on these titles can be consulted in the following websites:

Https://narrativaoscarrigiroli.wordpress.com/

and

Https://louisforestiernarrativa.wordpress.com/[1]

THE READER IS KINDLY invited to consult them in the certainty of finding good reading experiences.

---

1. https://louisforestiernarrativa.wordpress.com/